RUNAWAY ROYAL

WENDI ZWADUK

Runaway Royal
ISBN # 978-1-83943-964-3
©Copyright Wendi Zwaduk 2021
Cover Art by Erin Dameron-Hill ©Copyright March 2021
Interior text design by Claire Siemaszkiewicz
Totally Bound Publishing

Whip It Up: Honey and Decadence
Lasso Lovin': Tying One On
Wild After Dark: Taken In
Boots, Chaps and Cowboy Hats: Between Us
Three's a Charm: A Sinful Tune
Sensory Limits: Just You and Me

Seasonal Collections
Heart Attack: Over My Head
Haunted By You: Miss Me Baby
Wanton Witches: Candlelit Magic
Jolly Rogered: Ruined by the Pirate
Naughty or Nice?: Wrapped in Red and Green

RUNAWAY ROYAL

Dedication

For JPZ, my prince

Chapter One

"I can do this." Princess Catherine shored up her courage. She was a royal. A princess. She could do anything she set her mind to—except stand up to the king and queen.

She stared at her reflection in the mirror. Her parents, the king and queen of Lysianna, wouldn't allow her to head to another country on her own. They insisted she be an advisor to her brother, the future king. Charlie could handle himself and he'd be a great king—whenever the time came.

If she didn't practice what she wanted to say, she'd flounder and this was not the time to lose her nerve. She tucked her hair behind her ears. "Mother, Father, I need to speak with you. I've completed two years of online schooling towards a degree in art history and I'm going to Kenton State College in the United States to finish it." Did she sound convincing enough?

She'd already completed her application for acceptance on campus, chosen her classes for the first semester and landed a good apartment in a building just across from the main portion of the campus. Her plane ticket had been paid for and she'd packed most of her things. All she needed to do was tell her parents she'd be leaving.

She abandoned her image in the mirror and resumed packing the last of her things—her brushes, photos and stuffed rabbit in her bag. She'd come back, but she wasn't sure when. Sadness filled her mind. Change would be hard—she'd only ever lived in the castle—but she needed to move forward with her life. She'd never be happy living as part of the court. Even if she did nothing more than teach an art class or run a portion of a museum back home, she'd be happy and doing something with her life.

Her lady-in-waiting, Corinne, hurried into the room. "I guess you're ready to go." She folded her arms. "Want me to go with you? I should."

She had plans for her lady and wasn't about to disclose them now. Corinne was terrible with secrets and would've told her parents before the point of no return. "It's handled."

Corinne sat on the bed. "What am I going to do with myself? I have nothing to do if you're not here. They might let me go."

"They won't." She closed her bag. "They like you. If my brother wasn't gay, they'd have married you off to him by now."

"But he *is* gay." Corinne groaned. "Sucks."

Her lady hadn't been shy about her crush on Charlie. In the whole of their time together, Corinne had insisted to Catherine she wanted to marry Charlie. The problem? Besides Charlie being gay, he wasn't going to marry Corinne simply to make an heir. He refused to change just for the royal line.

"Your parents would rather you marry Duke Elmore. He's handsome," Corinne said. "If you're into older guys."

Catherine shivered. "Older isn't the half of it. He's almost twenty years older than me, he's not handsome at all and I don't like him. I don't want to be married to someone who sees me as a ticket to the good life. He wants a title beyond duke." Her stepmother would never understand. She'd married the king, despite their ten-year age difference, just to have a title.

"So you're going to America to avoid him?"

"No." She simply refused to marry someone out of duty, not love. "I want to finish my degree. Art makes me happy. Him? Not so much."

"Well, it's time to talk to your parents." Corinne walked with her to the corridor. "Need me to do anything?"

"Nope. I've got this handled." Catherine gave her bag to the butler. "Thank you." She shored herself up again and headed down to the throne room. The car was ready and once she reached the airport, the plane would be waiting to whisk her to the States. Even if her parents said no, she'd left nothing to chance.

"Catherine." Her stepmother, Eloise, closed her book. "You look determined. Have you made a decision concerning the duke?"

"I have." She clasped her hands together. "I refuse to marry him." She stood tall. "I've made a choice about my future, too."

"Oh?" Her father finally looked up from his paperwork. "What have you decided?"

She sucked in a ragged breath, then sighed. "Mother, Father, I'm attending college."

Her father tipped his head and said nothing. Her stepmother gasped. "Why? You're a royal. You don't have to do *schooling*. Elmore will take care of you and you can play with your art all you want. Royals don't dirty their hands with studies."

Her stepmother spit the words out like sour candies. Catherine didn't care. She had to focus. "I want a degree in art history. I'd like to learn about the art here in Lysianna and around the world—like my mother used to know."

"Interesting," her father said. He tapped his pen on the table. "Why do you want to follow in your mother's footsteps?"

She'd prepared for this question. "I need to have something that's mine. I love art and I'm dying to continue my studies." She had to keep her explanation short and sweet. The more she talked, the greater the chance her parents would coerce her to change her mind. "I want something to hold on to that reminds me of my mother. I don't remember her and this is my private link."

"She's gone," her stepmother snapped.

"Let her have this, Queen. It's her choice," her father said. "She'll get bored after a year or she'll find this is the thing she wants to do. As for Elmore, he can wait. Or maybe he can't and he'll choose someone else. Doesn't matter to me. He's a pest."

She wasn't going to get bored, but if her father thought Elmore was a pest, then why try to palm her off on him?

"What about Charles?" her stepmother said. "He should be the one to go first. Yes, he deserves a degree."

"He already has one." Catherine gritted her teeth. Their parents didn't know Charlie well. He hated being referred to as Charles and he wasn't interested in going to college again. Charlie had attained a degree on his own and had his plan for making his own way without their parents to intervene. Now was her chance to do the same.

"Anyway, I'm leaving." She turned on her heel and left the room. If she looked back, she risked changing her mind. Only forward now.

"You're what?" Her stepmother chased after her. "You cannot. We need to arrange lodgings and security and everything else. You'll need handlers and Elmore should accompany you for protection. Or he should set up a security detail so he can keep you safe, but stay here to run his businesses."

God, no. Catherine headed through the foyer to the waiting car. "Goodbye, Mother." The idea of calling her stepmother Mother annoyed her. She'd had a mother and the queen wasn't a very good substitute.

"Catherine." Her stepmother caught up to her. "We'll summon Elmore. You cannot make the flight unprotected."

She sighed. "He's old enough to be my father and he's not attractive, so no." She tossed her bag onto the seat. "I'll be fine. No one in the United States knows me, so I won't need the huge protection you're planning." She'd have her roommate in her new apartment and a few transplanted palace security guards around, but out of sight.

"Take Corinne, please?" Her stepmother pushed Corinne at her. "You can't go alone. And don't forget, you need to have an approved consort by the time of your official portrait reveal."

"Fine." Catherine nodded to her lady-in-waiting. "Let's go." She ducked into the car without bothering for hugs or kisses from her stepmother. That wasn't her stepmother's style. Her father hadn't left the throne room. Her stepmother glared at her, but didn't otherwise show emotion. She wouldn't dare. Any bit of cracking might show she was human and the people of Lysianna didn't think she had emotions. She wanted to say goodbye to her brother, but he wasn't even in the country.

Catherine settled on the seat and sighed. "That worked out exactly as I planned."

"What about me?" Corinne asked. "You said I'd stay here."

"I lied." She winked. "I couldn't go totally alone. They're right. I do need someone with me that I can trust." Well, mostly trust. "I packed you a bag and added your name to the charter. You're flying with me."

Corinne's eyes widened. "My princess." She grinned. "Naughty."

She sighed again. "I've never been naughty a day in my life. Crafty, maybe, but never naughty."

"You've lived in your brother's shadow for too long."

"He'll be king and I won't hold the throne. Even if something happens to him, they won't let me be queen, so why not have something that's mine?" Catherine asked. "I don't mind." She didn't. "This way I'm out from under their thumb and can experience life." She couldn't wait for the next Chapter to start. There was a great big world out there just waiting for her to explore it.

There was the tricky thing about her needing a consort, but she had plenty of time. The portrait reveal wasn't for another year. The world wouldn't wait a year—not when her consort might be out there somewhere.

* * * *

Twelve hours later, Catherine stepped through the doorway of her apartment. Picking an apartment had been harder than she'd thought and the one she'd ended up with looked nothing like the photos online. The carpets weren't pretty beige, but more of a dirty tan. The furnishings already there looked tired, rather than like antiques. The walls were boring and bland, but it was bigger than most of the apartments in the building.

Besides, she'd made it. The flight hadn't been bad, although the miles of paperwork had sucked. Then there had been moving things into the apartment. At least there had been an elevator. She'd never changed residences before and had no idea how hard lugging her bags and other belongings would be. Still, she'd done the work with little help.

Count one victory for me.

She deposited her personal belongings on her new bed. The art in the bedroom left something to be desired, but she'd live. Soon, she'd be so engrossed in learning she wouldn't have time to complain about the sad art. She arranged her brushes and makeup on the counter in the bathroom, then pieced through her clothes hanging in the closet. She'd run away from her life—away from everything she knew. On one hand, she'd made a huge gamble that could bite her hard in the ass. On the other, she could find the direction she needed in life. Direction was good.

When Catherine returned to the living room, Corinne had collapsed on the couch. "What a day." Corinne propped her feet on the coffee table. "This is why we left the castle? It's furnished, but it's lived-in. Couldn't you find something better?"

"I could've, but I wanted the authentic college experience." Excitement ratcheted up in her brain. "I've never done anything like this—nothing on my own. But I did. I'm here." She stepped out to the miniscule balcony. There was no privacy, but she was high enough up to be safe from stalkers. Did anyone care that she'd come to America? Probably not. She hadn't announced anything on social media and as far as she knew, her stepmother hadn't alerted the media yet.

She spotted movement in her peripheral vision. A man stood on one of the other balconies. Two floors down and one unit over, if she wasn't mistaken. Tall, dark hair...he could be handsome if she saw him from the front. He could also be nothing like she preferred. He sat on a weathered lawn chair with his back to her and bent over what appeared to be a drawing board. She couldn't quite make out what he'd drawn on the paper or board.

She almost shouted to him to ask what he'd sketched. Instead, she leaned over the railing and watched him. Within seconds, she recognized the form—a nude woman. He must have a girlfriend there. Or a model.

Figures. He had to be handsome and most likely taken. All the good-looking ones were involved with someone. She ducked back into the apartment and closed the screen door.

"Did you see something?" Corinne asked. She hadn't left her spot on the couch. "Anything good?"

"No." Catherine leaned on the doorframe. He could be good and handsome, or rotten. What did she know? She left the door and sat beside her lady. "It's strange how it's so quiet."

"Because there's no one around?"

"And because there's not someone breathing down my neck. My stepmother is desperate for me to marry the duke," Catherine said. "Doesn't she know I can't stand him? I've told her as much. Yet, she seems to think that she's got to push him at me."

"Still?" Corinne shrugged. "He's not so bad."

"Yeah, he is." He'd tried to assault her at the last ball and demanded she marry him before she did something stupid, like lose her virginity to someone else. Her stomach lurched. She'd rather die than marry him. "At least we're here where he'll leave me alone. I think he's trying to curry my father's favor and it doesn't appear to be working."

"Everyone wants to curry his favor."

"Maybe that's my problem," Catherine said and left the sofa. "I don't want to curry my father's favor. He doesn't know what to do with me." She faced her lady. "The other issue is that I don't have enough authentic people in my life. Everyone seems to want to know a princess or wants to get their sticky hands on the title. No one ever asks me what I like or if I have thoughts on things."

Corrine crossed her ankles. "You're a princess, honey. It's going to be hard."

"I know."

"But I get what you mean." Corinne stood, then hugged Catherine. "It's hard to get to know you when your stepmother lurks, Elmore hangs on and you're not alone. It's also difficult because you're right, no one ever asks you what you want out of life."

"I know," she said. She rested her head on Corinne's shoulder and closed her eyes. Her life had become more complicated. *Time to start working on the next steps.* She opened her eyes. "So, we need a cover story."

"We do?"

"Yes, and I've been thinking about what we should say. You're my older sister — older by two years — and we're living together to save money." Catherine nodded. "I'm finishing my degree and you're working."

"I am working—as your lady—and I am two years older." Corinne frowned. "Are you sure this is going to work?"

"Nope." She paced the length of the apartment. "So, you're my sister and we're here so I can finish school. You'll still be Corinne, but I'll go by my middle name—Zara—just in case anyone thinks they've figured out who I am."

"Zara?"

"Uh-huh." She rubbed her hands together. "Why? What's wrong with my middle name?"

"Nothing. I'm just not used to using it." Corinne shrugged. "You know this is the smartest thing you've ever done."

"Is it?" She hadn't expected Corinne to say such a thing. "You usually talk me out of stuff."

"I do, but this is different. You're out, you're experiencing life and you've taken charge. It's what a leader does and I'm proud of you." Corinne hugged her again. "I'm also tired. See you in the morning?"

"Sure. I'd like to look around campus, so I'll probably head out early for a walk. It's not weird to want to look around, right?" Catherine asked. She had to be Zara. If she wanted to be described by a new name, then she had to act that way.

"By yourself?" Corinne stopped short. "You can't do that."

"You do realize I'll have to go to class alone, right?" She'd have her security out of sight but within reach if she needed it.

"I guess you will, but it seems risky."

"I'll be fine, but I've already set up security agents—three that aren't attached to the palace—and I'll have my phone." She nodded. She'd seen the guards lingering around the building. If she were most adventurous, she'd make a play for one of them. Her father would have a coronary, though.

"Okay, but this isn't Lysianna. You can't scream royalty and privilege if you get a ticket or get into trouble," Corinne said. She frowned and rested her hands on her hips. "Be smart."

"I will." She sat on the sofa until Corinne left the room. Once alone, she picked up her sketch book and pencil before heading back out to the balcony. She left the door open and sat on the bare concrete. The world glittered below. Sure, there had been danger in Lysianna. People robbed one another and many lied. The same ones found guilty tried to appeal to her father for leniency. Campus life wouldn't be much different. People would be rotten to one another and they'd try to steal—boyfriends, girlfriends, supplies, grades... It was life and the world wasn't perfect, but she didn't mind as long as she had a chance to experience it. Her eyes were open concerning school, but she still loved the romance of being so far from home and meeting new people. The variety! Not everyone would bow to her and some might not notice her. What a concept!

She spied the tall, dark-haired man on his balcony. He held a cup of something. Coffee? Tea? Something stronger? She scooted over on her own balcony to watch him. He stood barefoot and clad in nothing but pajama pants. Was this his post-sex look? She sort of hoped so.

He wrapped both hands around the cup and rested his elbows on the railing. Worry knotted his shoulders.

She could see his face finally. He seemed handsome. Dark eyes and a killer body. Strong, muscled...she wondered if he'd finished the drawing from before and if he'd slept with the model.

She shivered. She'd never slept with anyone of the opposite sex and the times she'd slept with Corinne didn't count because they'd actually slept. No sex involved.

She opened her sketch pad and created a list.

While I'm at university, I want to:
*be kissed properly
*buy a cheeseburger
*see a rock band play a concert
*have sex & lose my virginity
*have sex with a handsome man

She tapped her pencil against her lips as she debated the next item for her list.

*to meet the tall, dark and handsome artist downstairs
*to model for someone (nude?)
*to attend a real party
*to fall in love

She snorted. Love wouldn't happen. Not for her. Before things got that far, she'd be found out. The law of averages wasn't in her favor. If her stepmother didn't tell someone she'd arrived at the college, Corinne would let the secret slip.

Still, she could dream.

Besides, the list was only one of dreams. It wasn't like she'd created a checklist to live by. She'd come to the college to get an education, not fall in love. Even if she wanted to be with someone and experience those aspects of life, she had to finish her degree first. She'd paid the money to attend and refused to waste the chance—even for love.

Chapter Two

Luke held on to his coffee cup and contemplated his life. His artistic endeavors weren't turning out quite the way he'd planned. Nothing seemed right. The energy in the drawing didn't translate or the luminosity in the painting dulled. His representations were great and resembled the models, but the pieces lacked spirit.

Missy stomped through the apartment. "You used me," she snapped. "You told me you thought I was special and you've tossed me aside."

He kept his back on her. From the moment he'd met her, he told Missy he wanted her to pose for him. Romance wasn't going to happen.

She joined him on the balcony. "Did you hear me?"

"I did." He forced his gaze to hers. "I also told you we weren't going to have a relationship. I'm not looking for that."

"Right." She narrowed her eyes. "You came on to me. You told me I was pretty. We kissed…" She waved her fingers. "That sounds like the start of a relationship."

"You kissed me." He leveled his gaze. "You found me at the Corner Bar and came on to me. I tried to tell you I wasn't interested and you wouldn't listen."

She cocked her hip. "Then why'd you let me kiss you?"

"I didn't have much choice." He snorted. "You threw yourself at me and you were drunk. Taking you home to your apartment seemed like the right thing to do. I never tried to touch you and I didn't kiss you again. All I wanted from you was as a model. I need to get this degree and my work into the galleries. I've wasted enough time."

"I'm a waste of time? Men." She left him alone on the balcony and rustled through the apartment. "You'll never see me again. Asshole." She slammed the door as she left.

He groaned and resumed staring off into space. So much for using Missy as a model again. She knew how to pose and could do so without talking, which made him happy. He preferred to concentrate when he worked, not carry on conversation. But she wanted to date and he refused to have a relationship with her. He'd been up front about his policy to keep work and play separate. No sleeping with the models. She knew the score.

He hadn't come to college for love. He'd arrived at KSU to gain his master's degree in studio art with a concentration on painting and photography. The galleries claimed he needed more experience and a broader portfolio before they'd carry his work. Fine and wonderful, except the muse had opted to go on a long vacation. His art had fallen flat. With no art, no jobs. No jobs meant he'd have to find something else to do with himself. Art was his lover and his master.

Damn it.

This was a new semester with new chances. Besides, he had one year left on his program. He had to knuckle down, not consider dating anyone…unless the right girl came along. Someone who could handle him being an artist and having strange hours. Someone who encouraged him to be creative. Art soothed his soul and after his ex-girlfriend, Jenna, had wounded his heart, he'd decided to keep love on a shelf.

He finished his coffee and turned to head inside when he spotted a woman on one of the upper balconies. The units from the fifth floor up were double occupancy and larger apartments. They were fancier than the lower ones, especially his studio version. If given the chance, he'd like a larger apartment, but the one he had suited him fine.

He watched the woman. Something about her seemed to call to him and he wasn't sure what. He didn't get a good look at her, but she seemed pretty. He admired her pose — deep in thought. She'd folded her legs beneath her and her hair obscured part of her face. He wondered what she was concentrating on. He didn't remember seeing her around campus. How had he missed her?

The itch to draw her overcame him. He picked up one of his sketch pads and inched over to the weather-beaten lawn chair. He could watch her without looking weird and could draw her. She wouldn't know he'd been inspired by her, either. Sneaky wasn't his style, but he appreciated people watching — especially her because she fascinated him. He completed the simple sketch in moments and added little shading. The drawing had life to it. He'd captured something within her. The light he wished he saw in many of his models seemed to radiate from her.

He was drawn to her. His heart hammered. The moth-to-a-flame thing, the magnetic thing…part of him wanted to climb the balconies and meet her. Or use the stairs. That might be smarter and would be less strange. Still, he needed to know her.

Was she an art student, too? Or a writer? He'd never drawn a writer. Could be fun. Maybe she'd been penning the lines to a great story or the elusive bestselling novel. She inspired him. For all he knew, she could be the one he'd been waiting for and the one he thought he'd never find.

So much for giving up on love.

The odds were rather long that he'd make contact with her, though, and he wasn't a gambling man.

Luke finished the sketch and collected his things before heading inside. He tore the drawing from the book and tacked the page to his cork board. He might not know the woman—might never know her—but she'd rekindled a spark within him to create and he needed the incentive. He needed to find the light again.

He could be mistaken, but he liked the way he felt when he looked at her and loved that the muse seemed to have come back.

Thank you, God. Without the muse, he'd be sunk.

He needed to meet the mystery woman and keep his muse happy.

* * * *

Luke strolled across campus on Friday and headed to the art building. He needed a new set of models and hadn't come across the woman on the balcony again. He couldn't use friends and wanted fresh faces. He tacked his notice on the model request board in the lobby, then ducked into one of the empty classrooms.

He needed time to think. He hadn't seen his muse since classes started. Damn. He wished he'd run into her because she intrigued him. Such a pretty girl and seemingly quiet. He didn't know her name, if she had a boyfriend or if she wanted to be his model. She might rebuke him. But after watching her the first night and drawing her, he swore she'd be a good model. Another woman had come out to the same balcony, but she wasn't his girl.

He wondered if she'd even talk to him. Would she like him? He considered himself handsome enough, but other girlfriends hadn't liked him being an artist. Jenna had hated the amount of time he devoted to everything but her. If he wanted to have variety in his portfolio, he needed to focus on his art. He'd painted plenty of still life and animals. He'd even done a few action scenes, but his strength was figure painting.

He flipped through his phone. So far, two people had applied to pose for him. One was a guy and the other a girl he'd already used.

"Excuse me?"

Luke froze. He'd forgotten ducking into the empty classroom. He looked up in the direction of the feminine speaker.

The woman smiled and clutched an art history book. "Hi. I think I'm lost. Can you help me?"

"Sure." He swept his gaze over her. Pretty. Her dirty blonde tresses were pulled back in a messy ponytail. Her cheeks were flushed and her dark eyes glittered. She didn't seem to be wearing a ton of makeup, either. He smiled. "Where do you need to be?" He tried not to stare at her figure, but *damn*. Curvy girls were his drug. She reminded him of his balcony girl.

"I'm lost. I thought this was the lecture hall, but it's not." She shoved a lock of her hair from her eyes. "I think I transposed the numbers. It's one-twenty-three, not two-thirteen, isn't it?"

"One-twenty-three." He put his phone away. "What time is your class?"

"Noon. It only meets one day a week here in the art building. The other class meeting takes place over in the gallery." Her blush deepened. "I'm not late, yet. Just lost."

"No problem." He left his chair. "I'll escort you." He grabbed his bag and gestured to the door. "It's this way," he said. "You're new here. Or is this your first art class?"

"Both." She smiled. "My other classes are history-based and at the Clinton building. I found those, but for some reason, I got my numbers wrong and myself turned around when I reached the art building."

"It's a strange structure. You enter what seems like the ground floor from all three levels." He walked with her down the corridor. "Which way did you come in?"

"The flat path." She pointed to the glass double doors. "There."

"Ah." He gestured to the open-plan stairwell. "Down here." He allowed her to go first and when he reached the bottom, he grinned. "The other gallery is over there and the lecture hall is here. If you come in through the grand staircase, then you'll be right at the lecture hall. Look for the carpet. That's how you know you're in the right place. See?"

"Well, that was a lot easier than wandering the building for the last ten minutes like I was." She laughed. "I got so nervous when I was on this floor that I walked right past it. I feel silly."

"It's a complicated building." He stood to the left of the carpeted steps. "Which class are you taking?"

"Baroque art." She smiled and seemed to gain a bit of confidence. "Today's the lecture."

"And Monday you meet at the gallery in Clinton for the virtual tour?" He'd heard of the Baroque class, but hadn't found the time to take it.

"Yes." Her eyes widened. "Did you sign up for it, too?"

"No, but a friend of mine took it last semester. Pay attention in the gallery because the prof is showing you the actual works used in the lecture," he said. "It's nice to see them in sort of person. At least you can put the art with the description."

"Thanks." She pulled the textbook from her bag. "I wondered if that's how they'd conduct the class. I appreciate the tip."

"You're welcome." He lingered another moment. He enjoyed their conversation and she struck him as a sweet girl. She seemed to be illuminated from within — or was that his libido finally waking from its long winter's slumber? "Do you draw?" he asked, trying to keep the chat going.

"I goof around with my sketch pad." She sat on the top step. "Join me?"

"Sure." He settled beside her. Something flowery swirled around him. Her perfume? He studied her up close. When she smiled, her eyes glittered. A dusting of freckles covered her nose. She fiddled with her book. Nervous gesture? He bumped knees with her. "Are you an art history major? My friend that took Baroque art was and he graduates this semester. I think he's doing an internship in the gallery."

"I didn't know that was possible," she said. "But yes, I am. I did the early work online, so now I'm taking the stuff that can't be done on the computer."

"Cool." He'd never tried online classes, but being a studio art major, it seemed useless. "You'll like Baroque art. The prof is good and fair." He liked the sound of her voice and her shyness appealed to him. The innocence could be an act, but he doubted it.

The lecture hall doors opened and a few students filtered into the foyer of the building. The girl tucked her book back into her bag. "I guess it's time."

"Just about." He would've liked a few more minutes with her. "I didn't catch your name." Not that he'd shared his with her, but still...

Her eyes widened. "I forgot my manners." She stuck out her hand. "My name is Zara. You?"

"Luke." He held on to her fingers a bit longer than he should've, but her hand fit so well in his. "It's nice to meet you."

"Nice to meet you, too. You are my knight in shining armor." Zara's grin widened. "I'll see you again, I hope?"

"Sure." He pointed to the message board. "Call me. It's my number on the request for models. I'm always looking, so if you want to sit for me, I'm game."

"As a model?"

"Sure, for my art. I'm a studio art major with a focus in photography and painting." He lingered. "Or call me if you want to hang out...or if you get lost again. I'll find you."

"Will do." She grinned again. "Bye." She headed into the lecture hall.

Something thudded in his ears. He smothered a grin behind his hand and walked out of the building. He hadn't heard the thumping in a long time. Zara did something to him — she made his heart beat again.

So much for his plan to stay away from women for the duration of his college career. She was irresistible.

Chapter Three

Zara paid attention through the class and jotted the necessary notes she'd need for later, but her thoughts didn't stray far from Luke. Excitement filled her mind. She'd not only met someone, but he was cute and around her age. She'd never considered herself awestruck, but he did that to her.

She focused on the notes and tried to forget him for a moment. The sheer volume of reproductions and information overwhelmed her. She kept up because she loved the topic, but she understood why some students struggled. Every time she thought she could catch a breath and a grasp on the topic, the professor surged ahead.

She gathered her things at the end of class and headed out of the lecture hall. The memory of her to-do list came to mind. She wanted to meet the handsome man. Was he the same one from downstairs in her building? He sure looked like the guy.

When she left the hall, she spotted the advertisement for models. He'd said it was his number and name on the request. She ripped the whole ad down and tucked it in her bag. He'd said he wanted models. The page echoed his comments. If she screwed up her courage, she'd call him and offer to pose.

Would she be good enough? If she were in Lysianna, she'd be forced to pose, but in some proper gown or ridiculous costume. He'd asked her to model, but what about when he saw her without clothes? He might decide she was too curvy or not pretty enough. Sure, they'd had chemistry, but it might end when she dropped her clothes.

Her stomach lurched. She left the art building, needing air. Her insecurities would be the death of her. Everyone loved Charlie. He was tall, blond, handsome and outgoing. He made friends with everyone and no matter how much he did or didn't work out, he looked ripped.

Then there was her. She liked her books, liked food, liked loud music and keeping to herself. She hated the ball gowns and kissing ass. She'd never be a good ambassador and would rather lose herself in research than try to charm people. She could still hear her stepmother chastising her for not being rail-thin or tall like her brother. Some people just weren't going to be statuesque or have Charlie's self-confidence.

She sank onto a bench beneath a shade tree and massaged her temples. Once Luke found out she had so many issues with her self-esteem, he'd probably bolt. If those didn't scare him off, her being a virgin might. Then again, she hadn't exactly been honest about being a royal, either. God, she was a hot mess.

Maybe she'd forget about him and he'd forget about her.

One could only hope.

She left the bench and made her way to the parking lot. The lot butted up to the soccer field, and a gaggle of men stood along one side of the field while others, shirtless, battled each other and kicked the ball across the grass.

She leaned against the fence and stared at the guys. So many sweaty bodies. She wondered what it would be like to touch them. Probably sexy. Would they be interested in her?

One of the guys glanced over his shoulder and must've seen her. He swatted another guy, then wandered over to her.

"Hi." He hooked his fingers in the chain-link. "I haven't seen you around here before. Are you new?"

"I am." She held tight to her books. "It's my first week on campus."

"I see." His eyes sparkled and a bead of perspiration slid down his temple. "Are you interested in coming to a party? We're having a team party tonight."

"Oh." She liked parties. "Do I need to wear a gown? Are we going to drink punch and dance to music? Or are we going to play board games?"

"Gown? Board games?" He tipped his head. "No, but you can wear whatever you want. I don't know about the punch or games." He licked his lips. "Just come. We'll find something for you and it'll be fun."

"We?"

"Yeah. The team. You should come." He winked. "I'm Tom and the team bunks in the Strasburg House. Can't miss it. We're at the end of Greek Row. Eight?"

"I'll see what I can do." She smiled. *A party. How fun.* "I'll tell my sister."

"Yeah, bring her along. If she looks like you, we can find a position to put her in." Tom waved, then joined the team again.

A position to put me in? Interesting. Guys sure say strange things. She walked away and one of her security team joined her after she crossed the street.

"Hi." She grinned. "I'm not in any danger."

"Actually, ma'am, he's not inviting you to that party because he wants to sip punch or dance. His motivations are more...sexual," the guard said. "I can't allow you to visit their house."

"They want to get horizontal with me?" She should've known. They weren't interested in her mind at all.

"Yes, ma'am." The guard escorted her across the grassy space to the edge of campus and her apartment building. "It's a whole new world here, Princess. It's not as innocent."

"I guess not," she said. "Thanks." She ducked into the building and her stomach soured. The guys might not be chivalrous like in Lysianna, but at least she'd seen handsome half-naked men.

* * * *

Tuesday afternoon, she ventured out to the balcony. Corinne had gone to the store and Zara needed the time alone. Her brain buzzed from all the information she'd learned in the past week. Being a student in person was turning out to be harder than she'd thought, but exhilarating, too.

She spied her mystery man on his balcony. Today, he sat shirtless on the lawn chair. Perspiration glistened on his back and she noticed his tan—no lines. She scooted to the edge of the balcony to get a better look. Her libido, what she'd thought to be dormant, reared to life.

Her mouth watered. If she could pick a guy for her wildest fantasies, it'd be him. He propped the drawing board on the railing and wiped his hand on his shorts. Was he trying to turn her on? It sure seemed like it. She pressed her knees together and heat engulfed her. Watching him seemed so decadent and wrong, but how could she ignore him?

The closer she looked at him, the more she thought he resembled Luke. Did he actually live in her building? Could he be her dream guy? The possibility could be real. But if she called his name and he wasn't Luke, she'd look ridiculous.

Corinne wasn't around and she wouldn't hear Zara make a fool of herself. Maybe she could utter his name and duck in case it wasn't him.

"Sure looks like Luke," she murmured. "Luke?" She slapped her hand over her mouth once she realized she'd said his name louder than she intended.

Oh God.

The man paused, then stood up. He glanced around a moment, then up in her direction. He shaded his eyes with his hand. "Hi."

"Hi." She waved. How could she ignore him, now that she'd garnered his attention? "Sorry if I scared you."

He frowned, then inched over to the left side of his balcony. "Zara?"

"Luke?" Her heart hammered. "My knight?"

He grinned. "It is you."

"And it's you." She leaned on the railing. "Funny to see you here." She'd been drooling over Luke. *Could be a good thing or it could be bad.* "How are you?"

"Good." He dusted his hands off. "You?"

"I wanted to sit out here and read."

"It's a good day for it." Luke folded his arms. "What are you reading?"

"A Chapter on Baroque art that concerns the early part of the movement." She'd forgotten all about the book. Why read when she could talk to him? "Want to get coffee?" She wasn't a coffee drinker, but she'd manage. Besides, she'd just asked him out...sort of. "You don't have to." She balled her hands. God, she sucked at flirting.

"I could go for a cup." An odd smile formed on his lips. "There's a common area up on the roof. I'll bring the coffee if you want to meet."

"I'd like that." This was happening. She'd managed to snag a date. A coffee one, but still.

"Give me fifteen minutes?"

"Sure." She almost said he could come as he was — shirtless. "I'll be there."

He nodded, then ducked into his apartment.

She hurried inside and bit back a whoop. She'd be meeting with someone — not Elmore — and could keep flirting. At least she could practice her flirting techniques. She stopped by the mirror and checked her hair. Wisps of hair had come loose from her ponytail and her makeup had smudged. She should fix both, but chose to only touch up her face. She wanted to be accepted as a person, not a royal.

She changed her blouse, then debated changing again. There was looking nice and trying too hard. The best attempt to be her true self-involved not having quite so much polish.

She grabbed her keys and left the apartment. She made sure she locked the door behind her and had the key in hand before making her way up to the roof. She hadn't known about the common area. As she twisted the handle for the roof, she hoped she was going to an actual place and not about to get locked out.

Then again, getting locked out with Luke might not be so bad.

She opened the door to the roof. The orange brick walls stood high enough to provide safety and still a decent view of the campus. Faded patio chairs had been arranged on a thick carpet of equally faded fake turf grass. A couple of umbrella tables had been set up, too. With a little work, the space could be more inviting. Still, the quiet settled around her and she relaxed. "Neat," she murmured. "A little oasis."

The door opened behind her and she tensed, then glanced over her shoulder. Luke ventured onto the roof. He held a carafe and two mugs.

"Hi," she managed. "Let me help." She took the cups from him. "Thanks."

"Thank you." Luke nodded to one of the tables. "We'll go there."

"Sure." She followed him across the roof. "It's nice up here. Why don't they mention it when you sign the lease?"

"It's not widely discussed." He put the carafe down before he moved two chairs over. "My lady."

She stared at him. He couldn't know about her royal blood. It wasn't possible. She'd kept her secret close.

"I thought we were running with the knight thing." A sheepish grin curled his lips. "Don't knights say 'my lady' to pretty girls?"

She caught herself. She'd called him her knight in shining armor. *Duh.* "They do." *Wait.* He thought she was pretty? Or was he putting her on? "I guess you do."

"See?" His grin regained strength. "This is what I get for trying to be smooth." He gestured to the chair. "Sit. I'll pour."

"Thanks." She sat across from him. "Have you lived in this building long?"

"A year." He poured the coffee. "I got in at the last minute last year at the end of the academic calendar. It's a nice place to live and I can't see moving a bunch of times when I have another year to go on my degree."

"Makes sense." She toyed with the cup. If she played with the mug enough, maybe he wouldn't notice her not drinking the coffee.

"Why'd you pick this building? You could live anywhere," he said. "I have to confess, it's a safe building. There's the doorman, although he's old as dirt and doesn't always pay attention. Then there's the keycards—unless you accidentally demagnetize them, they're good. People tend to keep to themselves, too."

She wanted to blend in. "That's why I picked it—safety."

"Do you have a roommate?"

"Me?" Not exactly. More like a handler. "My sister, Corinne."

"Ah. I thought I saw her on the balcony. What's her major?"

She never should've made up the story about Corinne or lied about her identity, but damn it. She couldn't risk being found out yet. "Finance." It wasn't a total lie. Corinne made sure the groceries were purchased and eventually would handle the transactions to pay the rent.

"Smart. I'm terrible with numbers," Luke said.

"So am I." She had to steer the conversation from Corinne. "I'm getting better with them." Now that she was on her own, sort of, she'd have to take care of herself.

"She's cute."

"Huh? Corinne?" She pretended to sip the coffee. Corinne was cute, yes, but if Luke was interested in Corinne, then why was he wasting her time? To get to Corinne?

"Yeah." He propped his feet on a nearby chair. "She likes to stand on the balcony with her coffee. I see her in the morning when I'm painting."

She stared at his legs. He had long ones and she liked tall men. His shirt pulled tight against his chest, showing off his muscles. He wore running shoes with low socks. She'd never considered the sporty look sexy, but on him, it worked.

"She's cute. I'll bet you're both getting the door knocked down by all the guys coming to call." He held on to his mug.

"Not exactly." Corinne might be meeting people, but she wasn't sure. "They aren't coming out of the woods to talk to me." She'd smiled at a couple of guys and waved to another, but none seemed interested. None, except Luke and she wasn't even sure about him.

"Why not?"

Shit. She didn't want to talk about her issues. "Corinne isn't dating. Do you like her? I can tell her you do."

Luke frowned. "Don't you like coffee?"

She sipped it and tried to hide her revulsion. "It's good."

"Liar." He put his cup down. "You aren't a coffee drinker. If you were, you'd have jumped right into that cup and given me a report about it. You've barely touched the drink and you keep changing the subject. Are you okay?"

"I'm good." She shouldn't lie. "I'm not a coffee girl, sorry. It seemed like a good way to get to spend time with you. I'm not that great at flirting and talking to guys, so lesson learned. I'll be honest with you and everyone else next time."

"It's okay." He reached across the table and squeezed her fingers. "Coffee isn't my thing, either, but it keeps me awake when I need to pull an all-nighter to paint."

Her skin tingled at his touch. She wanted this moment to last forever. No one had made her feel this important and like she glowed from within. "Do you go all night often?" At least she'd found her voice, but she'd asked a silly question. Judging by the way he tipped his head and pressed his lips together to hide a smile, she'd asked the *wrong* question.

"I can go all night, if that's what you're asking." He chuckled. "But you mean painting. I do with that, too, when I need to."

Oh God. She'd made a sexual advance... She closed her eyes. "I'm sorry. That wasn't right. I mean...do you paint all night? Do you — I need to stop talking." She opened her eyes. "I'm so not good at flirting."

"You're doing fine." He laughed again. "There's no wrong way to flirt with me." He rubbed her hand. "Don't sweat it."

"Yeah." Except she'd embarrassed herself. "Where were we? The paintings?" She cleared her throat. "Do you paint all night?" The words sounded okay, but her cheeks burned and she wanted to hide her face.

"When one of my paintings isn't working and I have a deadline close, then I do." He kept hold of her fingers. "You've probably had some, haven't you?"

"Some what?" She froze. "Deadlines? Or *some*?" She wanted some with him.

"All-nighters." He offered her the lopsided smile again. "We'll get you up to speed on flirting. You keep stepping into innuendo and don't realize it." He moved

36

the cup aside and crossed his ankles. "Are you okay, though? The first couple weeks on campus can be rough and you seem a bit lost."

No, just turned on and my lack of experience keeps showing. "I'm okay."

"Zara?" The door opened and Corinne burst onto the roof. "Oh my God. There you are. I thought I lost you or someone took you." She rushed across the patio space. "I can't… *Oh.*"

Luke let go of Zara's fingers and stood. "Hi."

"Hi." Corinne shifted her gaze between Zara and Luke. "You're handsome."

He'd said he thought Corinne was cute. Zara abandoned her coffee cup. "Corinne, this is Luke. Luke, Corinne." An odd sensation washed over her. Jealousy? A bit. Corinne was far prettier than her, taller with light blonde hair and blue eyes. Corinne possessed a welcoming smile, too. She'd be a better fit for the handsome man. "I should go while you talk." She pushed her chair in, then escaped into the corridor leading away from the roof. He'd probably asked her up to the roof to con her into introducing him to Corinne. She should've known. Guys weren't into *her* — they wanted the princess.

Zara didn't stop until she'd gone down a flight of stairs. She had three more to go before she reached her floor, but she had to catch her breath. Her lack of confidence would be the death of her. The guy she liked seemed to want someone else. *Story of my life.* Her parents liked Charlie better. Andrew had said he loved her until he found out she wouldn't become queen. Sawyer hadn't given her a chance once he learned she wouldn't put out. Both men had been pushed at her by her parents. Then there was Elmore. He only wanted a title. Why would Luke be any different?

Because she'd thought she could've been given a fresh start in a new place. No one knew her here and she could be taken on her own merits.

She sank onto the top step and tears slid down her cheeks. She wasn't angry with Luke—not really. Not even when he seemed to choose Corinne over her. No, the series of failures finally pushed her too far. She couldn't take her frustrations any longer.

Footsteps sounded behind her, but she didn't bother to look up. She hated when people saw her cry. Her stepmother would've scolded her—*royals only show emotion in public when it's joy. Never tears.* Sure, if she could stop crumbling, she'd stop crying.

"Zara?" Luke settled on the step with her. "You're not okay."

She wiped her face and tried to calm down. "I'm fine." She cleared her throat. "It's okay. I promise."

"Don't fib," he said. "You're crying."

"I'm overwhelmed, I guess." She needed to get herself under control. "Corinne's a nice girl."

"She is."

"Are you going to take her on a date?" She laced her fingers together. "She'd like that."

"Slow down and look at me." When she did, Luke tipped her gaze. "Corinne is a nice girl and she's cute, but I didn't join you for coffee to meet her. I wanted to meet you."

"You did?" It wasn't possible.

"Yeah. I enjoyed our conversation outside the lecture hall and want to get to know you better," Luke said. "She's cute, but you're fascinating. Besides, I like our non-conversational conversation on the balcony, too."

She almost said, *But I'm a royal.* Instead, she kept her mouth shut. He didn't know her truth and she wouldn't say so—not yet. Unless Corinne had told him and that was possible.

"When's your next class?" he asked.

"Four-thirty in Van Deusen. I needed an elective, so I took an introduction to metalsmithing course." At the time, it seemed like a good idea to learn how to make her own jewelry.

"That's a great class. I took it during my third semester." He nodded. "I need to go to the art building at five. Mind if I walk you to campus?"

"You'd want to go with me? After I crumbled like that?"

"I would." He bumped shoulders with her. "Why not?"

"I guess there's no reason we can't." She frowned. "It'd be nice." Being so close to him now, she detected his cologne—and the scent of paint on his skin. She looked into his eyes and noticed the flecks of green within the hazel. He had thick lashes and a nice mouth. So kissable. She wondered what he tasted like. Would he steal her breath with his kiss? Blur her thoughts? She wanted to find out.

"Zara?"

She blinked. She'd been caught staring at him. "Sorry." She'd inched closer to him, her mouth not far from his.

"Do you like the view?" He braced his arm on the step above and faced her.

"It's pleasant." What a ridiculous, noncommittal answer. She should tell him the truth that she was attracted to him.

He laughed and rubbed her shoulder. "Here I'm trying to be extra sweet and my best to be handsome, but all I get is that I'm pleasant. You know how to cut me to the quick."

"Sorry." She leaned on him. *I like you and want to forget the rest of my life for a few hours while I indulge in you.* She froze. Had she said those words out loud? If she had, he'd be either laughing or shocked. He seemed to be enjoying the moment. *Good.* She'd kept her thoughts to herself. "I should get my things for class."

"Sure." He stood first and held her to her feet. "I'll meet you in the lobby."

She nodded. "Thanks."

Before she could say anything else or fix her gaffes, Corinne appeared with the mugs and carafe. "You need to get to class," Corinne said. "And you need to take this." She handed the items to Luke. "This one needs to get moving." She nudged Zara.

"See you." Luke frowned.

Zara shrugged, but didn't fight Corinne. There was no point. The moment she explained why Corinne was pushing her along, she'd ruin her story. Besides, if Corinne wanted her to move, arguing was futile.

"I'll see you later," Corinne said and winked at Luke. She nudged Zara down the stairs, ending any further conversation.

Once she and Corinne reached their floor, Corinne grabbed Zara's arm. "What are you doing? You can't be out with him. What if your parents find out, huh? He's an artist. Your parents want you to be with someone worthy," Corinne spat. "He's cute, but he's no better than a peasant. You should have a husband who can support you. Someone who can give you the life you've become accustomed to. He'll never be able to do that. Sure, he's handsome and might be fine for an afternoon, but he's not forever material. You have to think about your future, the crown and your parents' wishes." She shook her head. "How will he support you?"

"Who says he will?" Who said he was her forever? Good God. She'd just met him. They might not be a match at all.

"What?" Corinne hustled Zara down the hallway to the apartment. "You're not thinking clearly."

"What if I want to date him, but I'm not thinking beyond a date? I have so little experience and he's trying to be nice." She folded her arms. "He offered to walk me to campus, not fuck my brains out."

"Zara."

"What?"

"Ladies don't talk that way." Corinne held up her hand. "He's a bad influence." She wagged her finger in time with her head shaking, dismissing her. "I never had these problems with you when you dated Andrew. You were so complacent."

"Because we weren't suitable. He wanted to become king when I became queen. Once he found out I wasn't going to inherit the throne, he left." She widened her stance. "I suppose you're going to bring up Sawyer? He jumped ship when he found out I wasn't going to sleep with him on the first date. I was sixteen. It wasn't right and he knew that." She held her ground. "Neither man wanted me for *me*."

"Luke might change his mind once he finds out you're a royal," Corinne said. "What if he's attracted to a plain girl and doesn't want a complicated one?"

She winced. Corinne was trying to wound her and it worked. "He didn't laugh when I thought he liked you over me and was trying to get to you through me." She wasn't sure where his loyalties were, but right now those didn't matter.

"He likes me?" Corinne's expression changed and softened. "He is cute." She nodded. "Do you think he'd go out on a date with me?"

"I don't know." Corinne's tone sure changed the moment she thought Luke might be interested in her and not Zara. "I need to get my bag so I can go to class. I'm meeting Luke in the lobby."

"Good." Corinne grinned. "Tell him I'd like to go on a date. Yes, I'd like that a lot."

Since when do I work for you? She couldn't say that. She wanted to be treated like everyone else. Still, she couldn't help but marvel at the speed at which she and Corinne had started arguing. They'd never had a disagreement before, but now that a guy had entered the equation, everything changed. Then again, she'd always gone along with what she'd been told before. Corinne might be her lady-in-waiting, but she held power. Now that the power had evened out, things weren't the same. "I'll see what I can do."

"Thanks." Corinne admired herself in the mirror. "Well, go. You don't want to be late."

"Right." She picked up her bag. She should be annoyed with Corinne but she had no ties to Luke. For all she knew, he could still choose her lady. She wanted him to pick her, but she knew the score.

"Bye." She left the apartment, then checked her backpack for her keys. She found the piece of paper Luke had tacked on the board to solicit models. Would he want to look at her as a model?

She'd never know if she didn't ask.

When she saw Luke, she would, and she'd accept his response with grace and dignity—like a royal.

Chapter Four

Luke strolled down to the lobby. Part of him expected Zara to be there already. Then again, part of him expected she'd ditch him. He'd bungled the coffee meeting by not thinking before he spoke. *So normal for me.* He waited in the foyer and debated his next move. He'd like her phone number and to set up a date. The moment he'd touched her hand, his skin had tingled and his world had shifted on its axis. No one had ever affected him in such a manner. She made his mouth water and his cock hard.

But she thought he liked her sister.

Not quite.

The longer he waited in the lobby, the more his heart sank. He wanted to see Zara, but he doubted she'd show. She'd seemed upset and he wasn't sure how to fix the situation. What had made her cry? Corinne? He wanted to make Zara happy, to see her and get her to laugh. He'd enjoyed their conversation and loved her smile.

"Luke." Zara hurried up to him. "Sorry. I had to change." She'd switched from her blouse to a T-shirt. "I forgot we're supposed to wear something that can get dirty." She edged her shoulder up in a shrug. "I'd rather ruin this shirt than that blouse."

"You look nice either way." He opened the door for her. "Have you been to Lysianna? I've seen it on television and in books but never been."

She glanced down at her shirt. "Oh, this." She blushed. "It was a gift."

"I have a few of those kinds of presents. My aunt went to Roswell and brought me back a shirt. It has big-eyed aliens on it." He fell into step with her. "So back to my original question—one of them. Are you okay? You're adjusting to campus life?" He wanted to put his arm around her to reassure her. "You seem unsteady."

She bumped shoulders with him. "I'm nervous."

"Why? I won't bite." Unless she wanted such things. He wasn't a novice in the bedroom, but he'd never ventured into fetish and kink.

"I saw the notice on the board. You need models." She stopped and brushed her hair from her eyes. "Do you have space for me? I'd like to model for you." She paused. "Unless I'm not right. You probably want thinner models or prettier ones." She shook her head. "No, I want to model for you."

"Whoa." He held up one hand. "Zara?"

"What?" She paled. "I'm not right for your models, am I?"

"I never said that." She'd make his wildest fantasies a reality because she fitted exactly what he wanted physically in his model. Her spirit and fire shone in her eyes and all around her. The innocence within her was something he wanted to capture on canvas. He grasped her hand and tugged her off the sidewalk to relative privacy under one of the maple trees. "I never said you weren't right. Why wouldn't you be good enough?"

She narrowed her eyes, then groaned. "Because."

"Because why?" He didn't let go of her fingers. He loved the way she fitted with him. "Tell me." He didn't understand. "Zara?"

"I saw the girl you drew. She's gorgeous. I saw you on your balcony with her and I saw the way you looked at Corinne." She rubbed her forehead. "I shouldn't have been watching you, but you fascinated me. Then I asked you for coffee and Corinne showed up. She's a better match for you and with less hang-ups."

He tipped his head and met her gaze. "When did you see me?" He wished he'd known she'd gazed at him before he'd spotted her.

"Two weeks ago. I'd just moved in and went out to the balcony to read. I looked down and there you were."

"Not alone."

"Not alone," she repeated. "She's a pretty girl. Is she your girlfriend? Or just a model?"

"Who says you're not pretty?"

She rolled her eyes. "You're avoiding my question."

"And you've avoided mine," he said. "She's not my girlfriend and never was. She served as a model. Now who says you're not pretty?"

"Me." She shrugged. "And other people."

"Corinne?"

"Among others."

"She's wrong."

Zara tensed, but held on to his fingers. "You're trying too hard."

45

"To do what? I'm telling you the truth as I see it," he said. "When I saw you on the balcony, you inspired me." He curled his fingers under her chin. "I don't know who cut you down—if it was Corinne or whomever—but they're wrong."

She stared at him, but said nothing.

"I don't know who destroyed your confidence, but they had no right to do it. You're captivating and adorable," he said. "I want to draw you, photograph you...see every bit of you. For me, art is about beauty and capturing it in all forms. You're beautiful in my eyes."

"I am?"

He nodded. "I made a sketch of you while you were on the balcony. I'm guessing we were out there at the same time, but never made eye contact. You were reading a book and I couldn't help but sketch you." He gazed into her eyes. The warmth and innocence melted the walls around his heart. "You might not think you're beautiful, but I see you that way. I want you to model for me."

"You're sure? You seemed shocked when I asked."

"Because I wasn't convinced you really wanted to do it."

She chuckled. "You're the first man in my life who hasn't pressured me."

"Then you're around the wrong men." He caressed her chin with his thumb. The softness of her skin and the closeness wrapped around his heart. "If you're sure, then I want you to sit for me. I don't want you to feel uneasy." He tucked a loose lock of her hair behind her ear. "I don't know who you saw me with, but you are beautiful to me and who inspires me to create."

"Thank you," she murmured.

"Welcome." He'd do whatever she asked to make her feel at ease.

"Whoever the girl was that I saw you with, you argued with her."

He knew exactly who she meant. "Missy." He remembered. He also recalled seeing Zara for the first time that afternoon. She'd watched him at the same time—just as much as he'd observed her. No kidding. He couldn't wait to capture her image in paint and photography.

"Missy reminded me of everything I'm not," Zara said. "She's tall, statuesque, thin and perfect." She squeezed his hand. "If you think I'll measure up, then I'd like to model for you."

"I know you do." He'd have one hell of a time keeping his hands to himself when she did pose for him. He wanted to kiss her and prove she was adorable. She intrigued him. "I should have you sign a release so we can get started." He'd been given a standard form to use before he captured anyone in one of his pieces. "You can read it through, then sign it."

"Sure." She smiled. "What else?"

"We'll meet after your class and discuss the details." He couldn't wait to start jotting down his ideas for her session. Hell, he wanted three or four sessions with her. "I'll buy dinner."

"I'd like that." She lingered another moment. "Got any tips for metalsmithing? To make it less scary?"

"Pay attention and use flux." He loved the crackle between them. The electricity could light up the sky. "Be creative and don't be afraid to try stuff. It's an open media just waiting for you to use it." Sort of like him.

"That's good advice." She parted her lips. Was she about to kiss him? When she didn't, he wished she had.

Zara let go of his fingers. "I should head to class so I'm not late."

"True." He wanted to hold her hand longer. Instead, he walked with her into Van Deusen Hall. "Where's your class?"

"Fourth floor." She lingered at the steps. "I'll be done around six-thirty."

"I'll keep an eye out for you and we'll get supper," he said. "Yeah?"

"Yeah." She smiled. "I'll bet you're a great artist."

"How so?" She'd only seen one of his sketches.

"Because you make me feel special—like I'm the only one around." She traced her fingers over his heart.

"It's not hard." But he was. "You're captivating." Was he embarrassing himself? He hoped not.

She blushed. "I'll see you here at six-thirty." She hurried up the stairs and out of sight.

Luke stood rooted to the spot for another moment. She didn't see her beauty and it sounded like she hadn't been appreciated. He'd show her he cared about her.

After a few seconds, he left the lobby. He should go to the studio and sketch out plans for the sessions with her. Before he started working, he liked to have an idea what direction he'd take with each subject. Plus, a plan would give him an outline to present to Zara. He didn't want her to simply drop her clothes and stretch out on his bed. There had to be a purpose in her modeling. What was she looking at? What was she doing? Thinking about?

He wandered out to the garden in front of Van Deusen. The serenity of the space wrapped around him. Zara would look wonderful amongst the flowers. Maybe he'd use the garden for photographs with her — clothed ones. He refused to have her pose nude in public. He perched on the closest bench and sketched out some ideas

"Luke?" Missy strode up to him. "You're out in the daylight. Are you okay?"

"I'm great." He closed his sketchbook. "I'm busy, too."

"Who is she?"

"Huh?"

"That girl. I saw you holding hands. Who is she?" Missy sat beside him. "Does she know about us?"

He'd never quite get Missy to understand he wasn't attracted to her. She suited him as a model, but nothing more. Her beauty worked well for his art, but her negativity shimmered around her.

"Well?" She crossed her legs and bumped his shin with her foot.

"There isn't an 'us'." He held on to the pencil, but didn't open the sketchbook. "Missy, we weren't ever going to work. I told you that."

"You liked me." She walked her fingers down his thigh. "You enjoyed painting me."

"I did." He wouldn't lie. She'd been a great subject at one time, but not now. "I need to get sketching for my semester project." He should have his plan for his paintings of Zara, too. He wanted to photograph her, too. Zara would be great for dramatic photos with high contrast and a sensual painting...he could see her on his bed, tousled from sex and happily lounging. Truth be told, he wanted to be the one who made love to her so that she'd be in that euphoric state.

"I saw you with her. She's young and innocent-looking." Missy crinkled her nose. "You'd better tell her you'll get bored. Once your *muse* gets tired of her, you'll move on. Say that up front and if she still lets you draw her, then you're lucky, but she'll probably dump your ass high and dry."

"I know." His muse could be fickle. When the muse decided to move on, he did. Zara didn't strike him in the same way the others had, though. He wanted to spend time with her without art being in the middle. He liked touching Zara and the innocence in her eyes. She wasn't like other girls. She didn't seem to be in the modeling game for the cash or anything else. He doubted she'd ever posed for anyone before. Maybe she didn't need the money or she genuinely liked art. He'd have to find out.

"You don't deserve her," Missy said. "You deserve to be treated the way you treat girls—like they're not important."

He groaned and faced her. She had the wrong idea and was hurting, but he hadn't done anything to hurt her. "Wait."

"I touched a nerve, didn't I?" She smiled and her eyes narrowed. "I thought so."

"Actually you did, but you're not telling the truth. We didn't date. I told you right up front that I wanted a model and nothing more. You blew things up in your mind, making us more than two people involved in making art. I never saw you in a romantic way and I tried to be honest with you. You refused to hear me," he said. "I'm sorry."

"Does she want to sleep with you?"

"I don't know." He'd thought long and hard about that very question and his answer. Part of him wanted to jump into bed with her right now. The rest of him thought he should keep some separation. Too bad his heart wanted Zara more than his head wanted to resist.

"Will she still like you if she refuses to sleep with you? Will you keep her around?"

"That's not a fair set of questions." He couldn't answer for Zara and yeah, he would keep her around. He'd become friends with her and enjoyed her company.

"Why isn't that fair?"

"You're comparing whatever might happen with her with what happened between you and me. "I never planned to sleep with you—like I always said." He tucked the sketchbook back in his bag. He'd jot the ideas down later. "We did great work together, but I need to create new art. There's nothing wrong with us as people, but as lovers, it won't happen. I need to go in my own direction."

"Without me?"

"Yeah." He couldn't be plainer.

Missy sighed. "If you change your mind, you know where I am. Good luck with her, but I know it won't last."

"Thanks, Missy." He still considered her pretty and smart. He appreciated the caution in her words, but she'd irritated him that she thought so little of him.

He debated his next move. Stay in the garden and try to sketch? Or take a walk for a while to clear his head?

He sighed. He should work on his plan for his project. Before the end of the week he was supposed to turn in the rough outline. The general structure was there, but he needed to fortify his proposals. He'd walk with Zara later. Right now, he'd draw and organize.

Luke opened his sketchbook to his second drawing of Zara. He'd captured her image from his memory and swore he'd messed up some of the details. Still, he couldn't help but smile. She called to him and stirred his soul. He'd never be the same and the art he'd create with her would make his career. He just knew it.

He remained in the garden until six-thirty then closed his sketchbook. His hand ached from furiously scribbling notes and his quick drawings to capture his ideas. No matter how fast he worked, he couldn't keep up with his own mind. The ideas came pouring out of him because of Zara inspiring him. He couldn't wait to see her. His phone beeped and broke his concentration.

He checked the notification—a class update for Painting VI.

He read through the updated project description. According to the plan, the class would only meet once per month until December and he was expected to produce four completed canvases, all with the same model. A series.

He could do that.

He swiped through to the homepage of his phone and accident tapped the photo album app. A photo of Jenna came up. His heart squeezed. He should delete the image because she didn't love him. She'd moved on and was married now. He should look forward and not back, too.

At one time, he'd told himself he kept her photo around to remind him of his past bad choices, but part of him didn't want to admit he'd failed.

Things needed to be different this time. He had Zara and a reason to work harder.

He tapped delete and removed the image. No point in living in the past.

"Hi." Zara waved and walked up to him. "Have you been waiting long? I'm sorry."

"No need." He put the phone away. "Good class?"

"Yeah. I got my first piece of brass and learned how to saw it into strips. I'm making a series of rings. I'll never be able to wear them because the brass reacts on my skin, but they'll be cool—I hope. I'm getting better with the saw, but I'm unsure of the welding torch. Oh well, I'll manage."

"Soldering iron."

"Yes." Her eyes lit up. "I knew I'd get it mixed up. Good thing there isn't a test."

"It's all new and you're expected to be a bit turned around." He gathered up his things. "Ready?"

"Yeah." She fell in step with him. "I met someone in class, too."

Jealousy hit. He'd thought he and Zara had something growing between them. He had to be cool about the prospective adversary for her attention or he'd push her away. "Yeah? Nice guy?"

"He seemed so." She stuck her hands in her shorts pockets. "I'm going to introduce him to Corinne."

"Corinne?" *Thank God.* "I got the impression you were trying to say you'd found someone for you."

"God, no." She laughed. "I've got enough problems. I don't need a boyfriend."

He'd like to change her mind on that.

"But Corinne needs someone. She's lonely and she's never had a boyfriend. Never."

"Have you?" He opened the door to the student center. "I thought we'd get something down at the Hive. There are booths and it's sort of private so we can talk."

"I've not visited the Hive. Actually, I didn't know there was such a place on campus." She grinned. "So thanks!" She threaded her arm around his. "You don't have to be so nice to me because I'm modeling for you. Be yourself."

"I am." His self liked and wanted to be nice to her. He escorted her down to the lower level of the building where the Hive was located. He liked how she held on to him. Having her beside him reminded him of escorting a grand lady somewhere. Who was he kidding? He had a lady with him. She was every bit class and grace.

"You're too good to me." She bumped shoulders with him. "I appreciate it because you're the one who makes me feel like I belong here. You make me feel special."

"You are." He opened the main door to the Hive. "We order first, pay, then pick the food up and select a table." He nodded to the menu on the wall. "Order whatever you want. My treat."

"I've never been in a place like this. I've only eaten in sit-down restaurants with full attendants." She stayed beside him and seemed to squeeze right to his side. "What are you getting?"

"A burger, fries and soda." He should get water, but he'd rather switch it up right now. "You've never gone to a fast-food joint?" Not that this was fast food, but whatever. Close enough.

"I'll have that, too. I haven't had a burger in five years," she said. "Since a visit to Colorado with my parents, but that place had tablecloths, attendants and a sommelier."

"Oh." A sommelier? He should ask more questions, but maybe she was pulling his leg. He placed the order and paid, then gestured to the waiting area. "Thanks," he said to the attendant. He turned his attention to Zara. "Were you a vegetarian?" Her dietary choices weren't his business, but the question came out faster than he could take it back.

Her eyes widened. "No. It just wasn't served…in my household." She paled. "Yeah, not in our house."

"Well, it should be ready soon. Where would you like to sit? Over in the corner is quiet." He directed her to an open booth. The music wasn't as loud and the lighting not so bright. "Why don't you sit there and I'll bring it over."

"This is perfect." She slid into the curved booth and after a few minutes, he joined her with their food.

She sat right beside him. "You probably think I'm strange, not eating hamburger."

"No." He withdrew his sketchbook from his bag. "You're fine." Sure, he had a bunch of questions, but everyone had different experiences in life.

She placed her hand on the book. "Corinne likes you."

"I know." Her quick-turn confused him. He frowned. "Okay, but I'm not into her. She's cute, but she's not my type, if you're trying to hook us up."

"I'm not and I didn't think so." She unwrapped her burger.

"Do you want me to be interested in her?" He stuck his straw in his cup lid.

"It might be better if you were." She shrugged.

"Why?"

She didn't touch her food and seemed to recoil from him. "You don't want me. I'm not right for you."

He frowned again. He wasn't liking the way the conversation had gone. "Because you're going to model for me? That doesn't matter. I've got plans and we're going to create fantastic art. I'm excited to get started."

"You are?" She toyed with her fries. "Oh."

"Yeah." He forgot about his food and opened his sketchbook. "See?" He pointed to his various ideas and explained his plans. "I have this vision of you on the bed, you're swathed in the sheet, but very naked underneath. Your hair is loose and you're relaxed. The lighting is soft and it's a romantic feel. Then the next one, your back is to the viewer and the lighting is more in front of you, outlining you. You're reading something, but it's not clear to the viewer what you're reading—could be a book or a love letter. The position of your body tells the story. You're hurting and sad because your lover has left. How long? The viewer doesn't know and has to read that into the painting."

"Wow." She nibbled on the fries. "Tell me more."

"There has to be four paintings, so I'm thinking the next one involves you standing before the window, but we'll set it up so that you're actually in front of the mirror. You've got the sheet around you and you appear to be pining for your lover. Maybe you're waiting for him to arrive for a tryst. Maybe you're watching him leave."

She wiped her hands and touched the corner of the book. "What about the fourth one?"

He fortified himself. "For the last in the series, you've got flowers around. Sort of scattered, like maybe the vase was thrown or the flowers fell from the sky like leaves. You're on the bed and appear to be sleeping. There's a letter beside you and the viewer doesn't know what it says. Are you deep in slumber? Has your lover left and you've cried yourself out? Or is it something stronger? You're thoroughly loved and exhausted."

"Or dead." She met his gaze. "I'm bereft because my lover only wanted to use me. He's gone and I'm inconsolable from being victimized. Instead of facing my problems and family, I've done my version of running away — for good."

She understood far better than he could've explained the situation. "Yes. What do you think?"

She traced her finger along the line of the quick sketch of her on the balcony — the one from his memory. "You drew this."

"You captivated me." He tucked her hair behind her ear. Sparks shot from his fingertips to his heart. He wanted to kiss her and being with Zara felt right. She could be a partner, not just a model or the means to stoke his muse.

"I did?" She stared at him and her lips parted. "Me?"

"You." The electricity between him and Zara swelled, making him forget about his dinner.

"Can we start this tonight?" she asked. "Like soon?"

She'd scrambled his brain. "Huh?"

"Let's take the food to your apartment and start tonight." She placed her hand on his thigh. "I want to."

"Zara." Things were happening at breakneck speed and in the way he wanted, but he needed to be sure this was what she wanted. "Slow down."

"I'm not going too fast." She nodded. "I've thought this through and I want to get started. Take me to your apartment. I want to pose for you. Nude."

Hell yes.

Chapter Five

She'd said the words out loud. *Holy shit.* As much as Zara feared he'd turn her down, telling him what she wanted felt right. She wanted to pose. She wanted to explore her life and sexuality, too.

"Don't you want me to model for you?" *Crap.* He might be changing his mind. She hadn't thought of that. Things were going so well.

"I do." He grasped her hand and tucked the food into the carryout box. "First, do you have anything to do tonight? I don't want to keep you from your work and guarantee this will take a while."

"I have schoolwork, but nothing I need to complete right now," she said. "I'll tell you if I have a conflict."

"If you have things to read, then I can incorporate that into the painting—I'll focus on another portion while you get your stuff done, then return to that part later." His eyes flashed. "You'll tell me?"

"I will." She helped him gather the food up and carried the soda cups while he took care of the box.

Within ten minutes, she and Luke were back at the apartment building.

Her heart hammered. She wasn't exactly wearing something sexy beneath her shorts and T-shirt. *Damn.* She should've worn something silky instead of sensible cotton. Still, she'd have him alone. She could test her allure. If she managed to turn his head, maybe she'd get modeling and life experience. She wanted to be kissed well, just like on her list. She wanted him to desire her. No one craved her for her own merits. They wanted the title she possessed and the money she might one day inherit.

She followed him into the building to his floor. The units were closer together and the hallway brighter. She hoped she didn't seem nervous and cause him to change his mind. She ducked into his apartment once he unlocked the door. The space was much smaller than her suite.

"This is my place." He closed the door behind her. "It's not exciting, but it works."

She glanced around the room. There wasn't any separation between the kitchen, living room and bedroom — just one big space. The only room with some privacy was the bath. Canvases had been propped against the wall and an easel faced the window. A television tray held bottles and tubes of paint. A variety of paintings and drawings cluttered the two-seat brunch table. Books lined the lone shelf and photographs covered the walls. His desk seemed to sag under the laptop, camera and lenses, plus the tablet and larger monitor. He had enough space for two people, but the fit would be tight.

"Where do you want me?" she asked. "Which one do you want to work on first?"

"Here." He placed his bag on the armchair. "Sorry." He withdrew his sketchbook. "I see you on the bed, first. You're reading and tangled up in the sheet." He pointed to the drawing. "Like this."

She nodded. "I can do that." She'd posed for a few royal portraits, but never nude. A thought popped into her mind. If she had another royal photograph taken, she wanted him to do it. Dramatic lighting, something in black and white...very glamorous, but stark. She considered the pose he wanted right now. He'd have a sheet around her enough that nothing showed unless she wanted him to see it. "I'll get undressed."

"Sure." He rubbed his hands together. "Let me draw the blinds. I want the late-day sun in here. I'll put supper in the fridge, too."

"Slow down." She touched his arm. "You're as nervous as me."

He sighed. "I am. You're going to be vulnerable and I'm scared you'll change your mind. I want you to be relaxed."

"I will be." She smoothed her hand over his chest. She'd seen him without his shirt and admired his body. Touching him was just as exciting as looking. So sexy, he stole her breath. "Oh boy." She couldn't think straight. "You should strip to your underwear."

"Zara." His eyes widened, then he smiled. "Yes. If I expect you to be vulnerable, I should be, too. You're smart."

She caressed his pec for a moment longer, pleased when his nipple pebbled under her touch. When she let go, she missed his warmth. "Be right back."

She ventured into the bathroom and closed the door. Holy hell. What was she thinking? She wanted to be naked with him right now—that was what she was thinking. Her mind raced. *Nude. With him.* She removed her shirt and chilly air caressed her fevered skin. She'd never felt so alive before. She never wanted someone as much as she craved him.

Zara unzipped her shorts and shoved both them and her panties to the floor. Her nipples beaded. No turning back now. She removed her running shoes and socks, then her bra. Her body tingled and heat engulfed her. She wished she'd done more with her hair than the simple ponytail.

She ignored her fears and grabbed the robe from the back of the door. She covered up, then ventured out of the bathroom.

"Hi." Luke stood with the sheet and arranged the bed. True to his word, he wore nothing but his boxer briefs. When he twisted and flexed to make the bed, he left little to the imagination.

Damn. Her hands trembled. "Hi."

"Can I do one thing?" he asked. "Please?"

"Sure?" She left the robe open. No one, save for her lady, ever saw her naked. She wasn't permitted to wear a bikini when the family went on holiday. At least she'd shaved the night before. The robe gaped, giving him a view of her cleavage and her pussy.

"Wow." He loosened the elastic in her hair, then ruffled her tresses. "Yes."

"Good?" Did she measure up?

"Very."

"I hope I match up to your vision." She dropped the robe, revealing herself. Time for the ultimate appraisal or rejection. She braced herself for his comments.

He shook his head. "I won't be able to paint you without taking photos."

"You won't?"

"May I photograph you?" he asked. "I want picture references to work from when you aren't able to model for me. That way you can hold the pose forever because it's in the photo. The images won't be seen by anyone but me, unless you allow me to show them."

What did she have to lose? She was already playing with fire. "Sure." She crawled onto the bed and allowed him to drape the sheet around her. Her skin heated. She wanted him to touch her. To declare he wanted to make love to her.

The front of his boxer briefs tented. She longed to stroke him. She had no experience with me and yearned to explore his body.

He cleared his throat. "Holy shit." He picked up the camera. "This usually isn't difficult."

"Because I'm not what you bargained for?" She refused to back down. "I'm adorable."

"Whoa." He knelt next to the bed, then laced his fingers with her and kissed her hand. "No, sweetheart. It's hard because I'm not usually this attracted to my models and struggling to conceal my erection." He smiled. "You're gorgeous."

"I am?" Would he kiss her now? Should she kiss him?

"You are," he murmured. "I've got a hundred ideas. Keep looking at me like that and this will be magic." He stood and adjusted the sheet. "Look at me like you're just waking up after sex. You're tousled, sexy and happy."

She had no idea how to do what he'd asked, but she tried to watch him with hunger. She wished she could sleep with him. She'd never been with anyone.

He snapped photos and moved around her. His erection seemed bigger and strained against his underwear as he inched back. "Now look toward the window."

The late-day sun warmed her face. Her nipples beaded again. She pressed her knees together. Christ. She craved him, his touch, his hungry gaze on her body, his loving words… He turned her on. The more she stared out of the window, the more she hated being a virgin. Who was still a virgin at twenty-one? She wanted to be alluring and worldly. To experience life and know pleasure.

"What's wrong?" He put the camera down and grabbed his sketchbook. "You look sad. Was it something I said?"

"Nothing." She couldn't tell him the truth—not yet. She needed to know he liked her without the title. "What got you into art?"

He settled on a small bench that looked like a backward seat and propped the drawing board against the upright portion. He tugged a bowl of chalks over to the bench. "I've always enjoyed putting chalk and pencil to paper. I liked doing little sketches for my friends and people realized I could mimic cartoon characters well. One of my teachers steered me to art class and when I sold my first piece, a fired clay mask, I decided to get serious." As he spoke, he alternated between looking at her and the board. "What about you?"

"I went to a museum and wanted to know about one of the pieces, but no one could tell me anything," she said. "I think the curator was out. "It was a Madonna and Child and I wondered why the little boy looked so sad. I wanted to learn the history of the piece and the frame of mind of the artist."

"Did you ever find out?" he asked and kept drawing.

"No. No one knew anything about it." She glanced over at him. He'd smudged chalk across his cheek. His hair slipped over his brow and as he tensed, his muscles defined. God, he looked sexy. Did he have any idea how much he affected her? She focused on answering his question, instead of ogling him. "I never did find out, so I decided to learn as much as I could about art. That way if I'm ever asked about a painting, maybe I can answer that person's questions."

He met her gaze. "Sounds like a good reason to me. I wonder sometimes what the artist is thinking when they make certain pieces. Like what inspired them to go blue or have a red period? It's not always clear and with the Old Masters, there isn't any information on their mindset."

"Exactly. Why paint that woman that way?" she mused. "Was the model really that snobby? Or was she shy? Was the child ornery or behaved, but making them look like trouble worked better for the overall work? I guess I'm nosy." She chuckled to herself. "I've been told I ask too many questions and want too many answers."

"Nothing wrong with that." He frowned, then tipped his head.

She wished she knew what he was thinking. Every time he frowned, she wanted to fix her pose. The sheet slipped, revealing most of the upper swell of her breasts. "How long have you been in college? How old are you?"

"I'm in my fifth year," he said and resumed drawing. "I'm twenty-two." He grinned without looking up at her. "I never asked your age. I guess I should've."

"Twenty-one. I'll be twenty-two in December." She toyed with the sheet. "Where are you from?"

"Where did I grow up, you mean?"

"Yeah." If she'd been asked last week if she'd be comfortable having a conversation in the nude, she would've been embarrassed. Now, their chatter seemed like the most natural thing in the world. He was easy to talk to, whether she wore clothes or not.

"I'm from the middle of Ohio. A little town called Crestline. Nothing happens there." He brushed his hair back from his face and smeared more chalk, this time on his temple. "My mom died when I was sixteen. A drunk driver missed a stop sign and plowed into her car." He paused. "My dad never quite got over her dying and he drank himself to death."

She gasped, not at the severity of his story or the situation, but that he was alone.

"Silly, huh? Drunk driver killed her and he allowed drink to take his life, too." Luke resumed drawing. "I've never told anyone about that. Then again, no one has ever asked."

"About them?"

He nodded. "I hate talking about my past, but you're easy to talk to." He sighed and dropped the chalk into the container. "It's not done, but what do you think?" He turned the board around, revealing the drawing.

She stared at his rendering. He'd captured her, but something more than just her. She looked beautiful. He'd added the sadness in her eyes and a leisured quality to her pose. She looked relaxed like she might have just finished having sex. "It's...wow."

"You're the wow." He wiped his hands on a rag. "Let's look at the photos. If there are any things you don't like or don't want me to keep, say so."

"Is this going to be all you need from me?" She wasn't ready to be done for the afternoon. Dark out already.

"This is only the first session." He sat beside her on the bed and turned the camera around. "I took twenty-five images at least." He pointed to the little screen. "I wanted to capture the details."

"You did." She barely recognized herself — thoroughly fucked and at ease. Instead, she was wound tight.

"Do you approve?" He elbowed her. "Or are you the girl who hates to look at herself?"

"I approve," she said. "And I'm not wild about looking at me." She touched his arm. The vulnerability within her overwhelmed her and she longed to break free from her good girl image. "They're lovely. Will they help your painting?"

"They will." He put the camera down and toyed with her hair. "You make concentrating hard."

"I do?" The sheet slipped, fully baring her breasts. She shifted enough to sit up. If he wanted to look at her, then why not give him the full show?

"You do." He bridged the gap between them and feathered his mouth over hers.

She whimpered. She grasped his shoulder and scooted onto his lap. Every nerve ending and synapse shifted into high alert. She needed him. Her nipples brushed against his bare chest. Electricity shot through her body. Her pussy creamed and she ground on the bulge in his underwear. She opened to him, allowing him to suck on her tongue.

Luke splayed his hands on her back, cradling her in his embrace. She'd never felt so cherished in her life. She straddled him, needing to feel every inch of him. His cock thrummed through the fabric of his boxer briefs and the sheet and she wished the barriers were gone. Being with him was dangerous and riding the wave of pleasure was sinful, but she didn't care.

He palmed her breast and flicked her nipple. She wrenched her mouth free and whimpered. "Oh my God."

Luke opened his eyes. "Zara." He stopped touching her.

"Right here." She wriggled on his lap. "Why did you quit?" She panted. "Luke?"

"We shouldn't do this." He held on to her hands. "We should stop."

"Why?" Her hair slid in her eyes and she couldn't shake her confusion. What had she done wrong? "Did I mess this up?"

"No." He kissed her again. "I don't sleep with my models and I'm so close to breaking my own rule."

"Oh." She bit back her embarrassment. She'd thought they had a connection. "I'm sorry." Where were her clothes? She shifted to leave his lap, but he held on to her.

"Don't be sorry." He kissed her knuckles. "You're too adorable to ignore. I have rules for a reason, but you're not just a model to me. We've only known each other for a few days, but it feels like a lifetime."

"It does?" He didn't know much about her—like her being a princess. If she told him that now, he'd dump her in seconds. Then again, if she found out that he knew the truth, she'd bolt.

"You stoke my muse." He pressed her hands to his mouth. "I can't just capture your image. I want all of you and you're not mine to have."

"Why?"

"You deserve better than me. I'm just an artist. I'm a mutt. No one exciting and you're beautiful. You probably have men vying for your attention all the time."

They weren't, but she wasn't about to correct him. "I don't want anyone else." She might as well put her heart on the line. "I want you."

Chapter Six

Luke tamped down his excitement. She wanted him. Holy fucking hell, he had everything he'd ever wanted in a woman in his arms, yet he kept pushing her away. He was in college to paint and draw...to create photographs, not sleep with his models. He should be capturing their likeness and spirit, not trying to capture her heart.

Besides, things were happening so fast.

But he didn't care. His parents had fallen in love in a matter of days and had been inseparable until his mother had died. The same thing could happen to him. Zara could be his destiny.

She kissed him and toyed with the hairs at the base of his skull. The warmth and softness of her body turned his senses inside out. He'd never met anyone like her.

A phone rang and he didn't recognize the tone. He frowned, ripped from his sensual haze. She tensed and her eyes widened. "That's mine," she said. "Sorry."

He wanted to tell her to ignore it. Why did anyone have to interrupt their moment?

She yanked the sheet around her and left his lap. She tugged the phone from her bag. A crown decorated the phone cover. The crystals sparkled as she fiddled with the device.

He'd seen plenty of covers and plenty of bling on phones, but he never would've pegged her as a princess type of girl. She struck him as more down-to-earth. Maybe she thought herself a queen…like a queen of her own domain. She'd taken the top spot in his heart rather quickly, too.

While she talked on the phone, he swiped through the images on his camera. He could use many of the images for a series. Hell, he'd only have to do minor fixes and they'd be ready for display. She seemed to know how he wanted her to pose and how to react to the camera. He admired her beauty, the light and creaminess of her skin and the sparkle in her eyes. Even when she was supposed to look less than perfect, she embodied alluring to him. He'd have to pose her again and couldn't wait for the next sitting.

She tossed the phone into her bag. "That was Corinne."

"Everything okay?" He abandoned the camera on the table. "You look worried."

She clutched the sheet and stared at him. "I need to tell you something."

"You've got a boyfriend?" He should've guessed. At least he hadn't slept with her.

"No." She scrunched her nose. "Unless you're volunteering."

He reached for her and tugged her onto his lap. She didn't have a boyfriend. *Thank God.* He'd become rather fond of her. "Do you want me to be?"

"I do." She smoothed her palms over his shoulders. The sheet sagged, keeping her modesty intact, but showing off a great deal of her bust. "I like you and I want to be your girl."

He shouldn't date her because she was his model. If things went south, his art would suffer. But he'd never been this drawn to anyone before. If she wanted to be with him, then he wasn't going to push her away any longer.

She placed her finger over his mouth. "Before you answer, I need you to listen to me."

He nodded. She had his full attention. "Talk to me," he said around her fingers.

"I need to be honest with you. I've never actually had a boyfriend. This is all new and I don't know what I'm doing—that's why I'm so clumsy at this."

Was that all? "You're just fine. Everyone needs to start somewhere," he said. "Just tell me why."

"I haven't been permitted to date."

Interesting. "Corinne? Won't she let you? She seems rather protective." And a bit pushy.

"She's part of the reason." The sheet slid down farther and he doubted she realized how much of her upper body she showed off. She toyed with a wisp of his chest hair. "The guys I have been expected to date aren't anyone I wanted to be with. They're either older or not someone I like or someone good for me."

He frowned. "Expected? I don't understand. Why is anyone trying to decide who you should be with? That's your choice." Even if she didn't end up choosing him, it wasn't for him to argue.

"I'm a virgin." She paled. "You don't like that, do you?"

"Zara." He let her words wash over him. A virgin. No wonder she had no experience. She hadn't been with anyone. Part of him relished the idea of being her first, but part of him worried he wouldn't be enough.

She fumbled off his lap and yanked the sheet around her body. "I knew it'd be bad. I knew I shouldn't say anything."

He paused. The conversation wasn't one he'd prefer to have in the nearly nude, but they'd have to talk eventually. He stood, then captured her in his embrace. "Wait."

Wildness and panic filled her eyes, but she didn't fight him. "You don't understand. I like you and I want to be with you, but I'm not like those other girls you've been with. I'm not good at this." She struggled in his arms. "I'll mess it up and you'll get tired of my fumbling."

"Stop." He tucked her to his chest until she stopped fighting him. If it took the rest of his life, he'd make her understand that fumbling and not knowing what to do wasn't bad. Hell, everyone had to learn sometime. He loosened his embrace enough to tip her gaze and force her to look him in the eye. "I don't know what your sister said and I'm not sure why you're worried about me not wanting you. No one comes into this life knowing exactly what to do in love. It's a mystery and we're all making a mess of it until we find the right person. I'm honored you like me enough to want to explore with me. We'll go at your pace. All you have to do is tell me what you want and we'll go there. I want to be with you. I want to photograph and paint you." He kissed her. He wanted to spend his time with her and even could see them growing old together. He'd never had those thoughts with other women, but she was different. "You make me happy and my muse sing."

"Even if I'm a princess?"

"Even if." She hadn't struck him as the princess-y type, but he wasn't going to argue.

"I want to be with you."

"I want you, too."

"You'll teach me?"

He wanted to be her only teacher and lover. "I will, but I have a request."

Her hands trembled. "Okay?"

"Just me." He settled on the bed with her on his lap. "If you're with me, then we're a couple. I don't want to share. Not in my bed, not in my relationships and not with my models. I'll teach you, I'll cherish you and you've got all of me in return."

"That's exactly what I want. You." She kissed him and let go of the sheet.

He moaned, consumed by her and with her. She was such a precious woman. So beautiful. He stretched out beneath her and allowed her to explore him, his skin tingling from her touch. His nipples pebbled and blood surged to his cock. He threaded his fingers in her hair as she feathered kisses over his chest.

She moved back to his chin and up to his mouth, then sucked on his tongue and caressed his pecs. The sheet slipped free, giving him complete feel of her skin on his. Being with her was so intimate and perfect. She ground on him and heat from her body seared him. As she writhed, she situated his dick between her legs.

He wanted to slow down, but the need within him overwhelmed him. He rolled them over, pinning her naked form beneath his.

She panted. "Make love to me." She slid her arms around his neck. "Need you."

"We have to go slow." He braced himself of his knees and slid one hand between her legs. So wet. He caressed her clit.

She whimpered. "Luke."

He liked her responsiveness. She came alive for him, not only in his bed but before his camera. He nipped her throat and continued to stroke the tender bud of her clit. She writhed and bucked beneath him. When he added a bit of pressure, she dug her nails into his shoulders.

He kissed his way to her breasts and sucked one nipple into his mouth. She tensed, then bucked again. Her liquid excitement increased and he eased one digit into her body. Christ, she was tight. He couldn't wait to sink into her body and make them one soul, moving together.

"Need you," she managed again. She tensed and squeezed her legs around him. "Please?"

"I will." He nuzzled her breast. He'd do just about anything for her, but first, they needed a rubber and he wanted to open her just a bit more. He pumped his digit in her pussy, then added a second finger.

Her legs trembled and she opened her eyes. "Oh, wow." She rode his fingers, simulating sex. "God, it feels good."

He kissed her belly, then slowly withdrew his fingers from her channel. "You're sure?" He shoved his boxer briefs to the floor, then retrieved a condom from the dresser. "Zara?"

"I want you as my first," she said. "Please?"

If he had his way, he'd be her only. God, he was thinking too far ahead, but damn, she intoxicated him. He tore open the packet and sheathed himself. Just his hand on his body had him right at the edge. This wouldn't last long.

She stared up at him. Her kiss-swollen lips, dusty-rose nipples and curvy body called to him. Her cream covered her pussy lips. He'd never seen anyone so sexy in his life. Part of him wanted to stop time and photograph her in this moment. He'd never show anyone the image—it was just for him.

Luke climbed onto the bed and settled between her legs. "Breathe for me. It'll be uncomfortable for a little bit. Just focus on me. I'm right here with you."

She fixed her gaze on his and nodded. "I trust you."

The weight of the moment settled on his shoulders. He wanted the act to be great for her. "Breathe, sweetheart." He caressed her clit as he pushed into her. So snug, but she was made for him. He gritted his teeth and leaned over her.

Momentary panic filled her eyes.

"It'll get better." He moved his hips and focused on her. "So beautiful," he murmured. "I love the way you're surrounding me, Zara."

She hooked her legs about his waist and panted. A shiver wracked her body. She fixed her gaze on him. Panic left her eyes within moments and she relaxed a bit.

"There you go." He kissed her. "Relax. I'm with you." He moved faster, pushing deeper. In and out, he became one with her. He couldn't think straight—just feel.

Zara held on to him. At first, she seemed scared, but fell right into the act. She met him thrust for thrust. Her lips parted, but no sound came out. She arched her back.

"Yes, baby." He nuzzled her neck as the orgasm built within him. His thoughts blurred. This wasn't just an act—they weren't simply having sex. With her, he made love. The concept blew his mind. He jerked forward as the climax hit. "Oh God."

She writhed beneath him.

Luke surged into her and rested his forehead against hers. He added a couple more thrusts, then stilled as the orgasm spiraled through his body.

She panted. "Luke."

As high as he sailed from coming, he wished she'd been able to come, too. He eased out of her and vowed he'd bring her to orgasm. A trace of blood dotted the sheets. *Fuck.* She really had been a virgin.

She stared at him. "I ache."

"You've done something new." He removed the condom and brought a towel over. He'd been given a gift in her trust and virginity. He wouldn't trash this treasure for anything. No way. He tucked her to his side and allowed her to rest.

"I'm floating." She rolled onto her side and buried her face against his neck. "I'm sleepy, too."

"Rest." He'd hold her forever if she desired. She'd inspired his creativity and made him believe love was possible. He'd fallen for her. Was it love? Too soon to tell, but he cared.

Her phone rang again, then buzzed. He picked up the device. "Looks like your sister wants you. Tell her you're sleeping over tonight."

"She always wants me." Zara sat up and brushed her hair from her eyes. "Well, shit. At least she texted this time."

"What's wrong?" He moved the towel. "Everything okay?"

"It's fine. My parents are coming to visit next week, though." She scrubbed the back of her hand across her mouth. "I should go back to my apartment. I guess my parents want to video chat." She frowned. "I didn't know they knew *how* to video chat."

He shrugged to hide his displeasure. He'd rather have her stick around. "I suppose if you're going to talk to them, you shouldn't do it in the nude." He sat up and gathered her in his arms. "I'm breaking my rule to not date my models because you're different. I can't take my eyes off you."

She blushed, but didn't hide her nudity. "I like you, too."

"Next time, I'll bring you to orgasm, too." He rested his forehead against hers. "You said you've never had a boyfriend. Well, you have one now."

Genuine excitement blossomed on her face.

"Come back when the chat's done." He smoothed a lock of her hair in his fingers. "I want to sleep with you beside me."

She sighed. "I so want to skip the chat." She picked up her phone. "Give me your number now and I'll text you so you have mine. We can send dirty texts tonight."

He liked how she thought. "Yes." His phone blinked with the new message. "Got it." He wasn't ready to let her go. "Stay with me. Tell them you've got a big test."

She hesitated. "Let me get a bag and I'll come back. My first class isn't until ten, so we can spend the evening...creating art."

"Yes." His thoughts exactly. "You can pose for me again and we'll have fun." He couldn't deny her if he tried. "I'm planning on working while you're gone, so just come back."

"I will." She left his lap and dressed. "You make me feel stronger and bolder, like I can do anything."

"You can." He had no doubt she could do anything she set her mind to.

"I guess I can." She grabbed her backpack. "I'll give you a heads-up before I return, in case you're busy."

"Doesn't matter if I'm busy. You're not an interruption." He wrapped the towel around his waist and followed her to the door. When she stopped, he kissed her. *Damn.* Now that he'd tasted her, he didn't want to let her go.

She hesitated. "I don't know what love feels like, but I've got flutters in my belly and I can't wait to come back."

"I can't wait, either." She was dangerous to him. She'd shifted his focus from art to romance. At least she'd helped him work the two into one thread. Still, she scattered his thoughts, too.

She left and the silence engulfed him. He leaned against the door. Up to now, he'd figured his life out. This year would be different, but he'd expected that. Then she showed up and he wasn't as lonely. He felt human, too. Like his troubles didn't matter. He wasn't just a struggling artist, but one who also happened to be in love. He needed to channel his emotions into his work. If he did, he'd be unstoppable.

Time to create.

Chapter Seven

Zara rushed up to her apartment. *A video chat. God.* What was Corinne thinking? She'd probably gotten lonely and wanted attention. Part of her appreciated Corinne being there—she needed the moral support. But the rest of her wished Corinne would find something to do. Maybe she'd set Corinne up with that guy from her class.

Once she found out what Corinne wanted.

The noise in her apartment startled her. She touched the doorknob and hesitated. It sure sounded like there were a bunch of people over. Did Corinne know that many folks already? She opened the door and the noise grew.

At least twenty people filled the apartment. Music blared and someone had a light flashing. What in the hell? Zara walked past the knots of people toward her room. When she opened the door, she gasped.

A couple, both half-clothed, were stretched across her bed and engrossed in each other. When she looked closer, she recognized the anklet. No way. "Corinne?" She dropped her bag with a thud, trying to garner the couple's attention. "What are you doing?"

Corinne sat up and fixed her hair. Her cheeks were flushed and breast heaving. She shrugged. "We're throwing a party. Isn't it fun? I met these people in the building and invited them over. It's a great time. I wanted to help you meet people on campus and the guys from the soccer team showed up."

"I see that. They've trashed the living room." She folded her arms. "I can meet people just fine, but I'd like to know why you're making out on my bed." She wanted some privacy. "I thought I had to come back for a video chat. I'm going to assume that's not a thing now? The party was the thing?"

"Well, your room was closer for making out and yeah, I wanted you to get to know more people on campus," she said as the guy left. He eyeballed Zara, grunted then walked out of the room. Corinne shrugged again. "He was cute and seemed to like me."

The smell of rum filtered around Zara. "He seemed to like you? The rum had nothing to do with it, right?"

"It might." Corinne pulled her shirt back over her head. "I wanted a good time and it happened, so I wanted you to join us. What were you doing? Studying something unimportant? You never let yourself have fun and this was my surprise for you. This is how college kids have fun!"

"I was already having fun with someone." Zara rested her hands on her hips. "I don't care if you're drinking. You're an adult, but why are you acting like this? And why are you letting them trash the living room? We have pay for the damages."

Corinne smoothed the wrinkles in her blouse. "You always get the attention. Everyone wants to be around you and he liked me. It's my turn to have someone look at me like I'm important, not just a *side piece*."

"Next time tell me you want a party before you throw it," Zara said. "I'm guessing the chat with my folks…was just bullshit?"

"Oh yeah." Corinne blushed again. "Oops."

"Corinne." She didn't have time for this. "So did my parents make contact?"

"No."

She groaned. "Fine. I'm changing, then I'm heading back to Luke's." She picked out a T-shirt for the following day's classes and a pair of jean shorts, then packed socks, a fresh bra and underwear. Nothing sexy this time in case Corinne asked too many questions.

"What are you doing?" Corinne shut the drawer for her. "Who is Luke?"

"The guy from the roof."

"The hottie?"

"Yes." She switched out her books and tucked her tablet into her backpack. "So?"

"What did you do?"

"We're hanging out. He's a nice guy and I wanted to go over to his place while you're having the party. It's a win-win. You get to have the party and I get to have some quiet." She tucked some bathroom essentials into her bag, then faced Corinne. "I'm an adult."

"You might be, but your parents will find out about this and you're going to get burned." Corinne held up her phone. "Look. They know." She pointed to one of the social media outlets. "That's you and him on campus. I didn't know who he was, but doesn't matter. This picture has Elmore all upset."

She grabbed her brush. "He's going to have to learn to live with his upset. I'm dating Luke." She shoved the styling item into her bag. "I need to go. I don't want noise tonight."

"No, you want a handsome man. Did you kiss him?" Corinne followed her around the room. "You're going to embarrass your parents. Don't you even think about them? I'm here so you don't make bad decisions. I know Elmore isn't your Prince Charming, but he's willing to marry you and doesn't seem to care you won't be queen. That's got to mean something."

She stopped in her tracks and her hackles rose. Corinne, the person who was supposed to care about and protect her, wanted her to marry a man who was willing to marry her even if she wasn't queen? What kind of friend would nudge her to do something so wrong?

"It's true. You don't have many prospects and he wants to marry you." Corinne folded her arms. "You could suck it up for the crown."

"I don't want to suck it up. I'm making my way, finding myself and I don't belong with him." She zipped her bag, then retrieved the cord for her phone. "I'm on social media in a post with Luke. Big deal. It's not like we're making out." But once Corinne found out she'd posed for him, she'd have a fit.

"Stick around." Corinne sank onto the bed. "It's not the same having a party without you."

"I wouldn't know. I've never had a party that's anything like that." Her parties involved formal invitations, fancy dinners and ball gowns, but no fun.

"Well, I kind of told the guy I was making out with that I'm Princess Catherine from Lysianna. I might have said one day I'll inherit the throne, too." Corinne shrugged. "It was the rum talking."

Zara's blood ran cold. Corinne had been her lady for seven years. She knew everything and could get Zara into a ton of trouble. "Then you clean up the mess." She grabbed her bag and stormed out of her room. When Corinne exited, she slammed the door.

Zara didn't bother to look back. She navigated through the people. The guy from her room stood by the main door.

"I hear your roommate is a princess. What a crock of shit." He laughed. "I bet you're the princess."

"I don't know what you're talking about." She left the apartment and gritted her teeth as she strode to the elevator. She tapped the button to call the car, but before the doors opened, the guy joined her.

"We've never had a real celebrity here on campus." He stood in front of the doors. "Is it you?"

"I said I don't know what you're talking about. She's my roommate, but she's been drinking, so I don't know what she's said." She fiddled with her phone, texting Luke to meet her at the elevator.

"A princess, eh? Mafia?" The guy quirked his eyebrow. "You don't strike me as the mob type and you don't look like you've come from money."

The doors opened and the car jangled. Luke stood in the corridor. "Hi, babe."

She ducked under the guy's arm and hurried to Luke.

"No fucking way. You are her." The guy laughed. "The picture was right. Nice."

The doors closed before she could argue with him, but she saw no point in it anyway. She sagged into Luke. "Well, that's messed up."

"What's wrong?" He walked her down the hall to his apartment. "What's going on? You're white as a sheet."

"Just a moment." She sent texts to the guards, reminding them to keep an eye on the apartment and Corinne, then to also put a guard at Luke's place. Her past had come to call and she couldn't hide from him any longer.

"We need to talk." Zara faced Luke. She shut the apartment door, locking them in. If she didn't put her guard down now, she'd never do it.

Her phone rang, but instead of being the guards, it was the royal number. "Damn it." She massaged her forehead. "Just a second. Hello?" She pressed the phone to her ear and hoped she hadn't turned the volume up too loud. She wanted to be the one to tell Luke the truth, not for him to hear it second-hand.

"What did you do?" her stepmother snarled.

"What did I do?" She massaged her forehead again. "I'm an adult. Whatever it was, it's not that big of a deal." Getting her picture taken while she stood in front of the building on campus wasn't worth her stepmother's ire. "It was just a photo."

"You've embarrassed the crown," her stepmother barked. "You've embarrassed us all."

Her head ached. "How? We were talking and nothing happened." Not in that moment anyway.

"You're dancing on tables and you've bared your chest to strangers," her step-mother said. "I've seen the photos. They're all over social media and you're trending for getting out of control."

"That's Corinne. It's not me." She sank onto the bed and rested her head on her hand. "Mother, you have to trust me. I'm behaving. I am." Tears pricked her eyes and she disconnected the call. Everything she'd worked so hard for was falling apart.

"I don't know what's wrong, but I'll try to fix it." Luke gathered her in his arms. "Talk to me."

She had to compose herself. *God. Being honest sucks.* "I need to tell you something that'll probably make you throw me out, but it's the chance I have to take. I lied to you."

Luke kept her on his lap and sighed. "Lay it out for me. You've got a boyfriend? Husband?"

"Nothing like that." She forced herself to look him in the eye. She could get lost in the hazel depths of his eyes and wished the world would melt away right now. "I'm a princess."

"You said that." He shrugged. "You're not as high maintenance as some, but so what? There's no shame in being needy."

"No." She left his lap and retrieved her ID from her bag. "See? This is my full name. I'm a princess."

"HRH Princess Catherine of Lysianna?" He crooked an eyebrow. "How'd you get the college to make the ID? Wait, it's a fake, right? Nice joke."

She shook her head. "It's real." She offered up her driver's license. "See?"

He narrowed his eyes and pushed both cards away. "You're putting me on."

"No."

"I don't understand. Who are you?"

The revulsion in his voice churned her stomach. "Let me talk, okay? I'll explain."

"Please do." He crossed his ankles and arms while sitting on the bed. "I'm listening."

She refused to cry or puke, despite her nerves getting the better of her. "My name is Princess

Catherine Zara of Lysianna. I'm the second child of King Martin and Queen Ria. My brother, Charles, will be the next king. Until three weeks ago, my only acts of transgression against the crown involved my love of metal music and my decision to take college courses online. I'm not the ideal princess my parents wanted and I'm not even the daughter they envisioned. Corinne isn't my sister. She's my lady-in-waiting."

He tipped his head and stared at her, but said nothing.

"I want to be my own person, which is why I came to Kenton. I used my middle name to buy time and earn my degree before the press realized I'm here. My plan worked until today." She fluttered her hands and sank onto the arm of the overstuffed chair. "I didn't want to lie to you, but I wanted to do this college thing on my own."

"What happened?" He didn't scream or raise his voice, but the brittle edge bothered her.

"Corinne, among others. She's telling the newly found friends she's got upstairs at the party in my apartment that she's me. I don't care that she's using my name if it gives her an edge with guys. She doesn't get to club and she's never had a boyfriend that I know of, so whatever. But she's acting out—dancing on the dining room table with her shirt off—and it's being posted on social media as Princess Catherine is acting out. My stepmother was alerted to the behavior and she just called to chew my ass out."

"She thinks you're out of control?"

"Basically." She sighed. "That and my parents have had a plan for how I should live my life. The requirements are impossible." She shook her head again. "Now I've involved you and ruined the work I've accomplished on campus."

Luke sighed. "I should be pissed because I hate when I'm lied to."

"You have every right to hate me and throw me out." She'd been dishonest with him and knew damn well what she was doing the whole way.

"Your story makes no sense, though, but I can see Corinne trying too hard to get attention," he said. "Where are the pictures? Are they just of her?"

"Not exactly." She switched over to the bed and sat beside him. "It's her, I guess, but also us." She searched her social media and found the images. "These are those." She winced at the pictures of Corinne on the table, Corinne with her shirt up, but her bra down and Corinne chugging what looked like a beer. Zara recognized one of the men helping Corinne off the table. "That's Ray. He's one of my guards. He's always liked her, so he'll make sure she's okay."

"Good." Luke rubbed her back. "Someone has an eye on her and you?"

"I have a bodyguard, but he's at a distance." She swiped through the images to the ones of her with Luke. "These are the other ones. I don't think my stepmother saw these. She's too busy being upset with the first set."

"It's us." Luke rubbed his chin. "Earlier today."

"Uh-huh. The media works fast." She curled into herself. "I understand if you've changed your mind about me."

He took the phone from her and placed it face down on her bag. "I don't know how to feel right now," he said. "Why didn't you tell me before now? Before she ruined the story?"

She refused to back down. She'd made this mess and she'd fix it. "I've never been wanted or pursued on my own merits. That's why I said I didn't date. The guys were really picked out for me. Who was a royal or had a title, who could handle being married to a woman who wasn't exactly princess material...who would lower themselves to being with me?" A chill ran the length of her spine. "I wanted someone to like me for me." Tears pricked her eyes again, despite her wanting to stay calm. "Sorry."

Luke pulled her onto his lap and kissed her temple.

"I needed to know you cared about me for me. I'll inherit money, but I'm not rich personally and I won't ever be queen. The best I can do is be princess or advisor." She wiped her face, but continued to look him in the eye. "Guys want what they think I can do for them—not me. I'm the ugly truth or whatever."

"They want to be king and think you'll get them there."

"Yes. They want me to make them wealthy and get them fancy cars. One guy told my father he'd accept money to date me." Her voice cracked. *Damn it.* "Charlie will be king, not me. But there are people who think they can curry favor with my father and others who want to bring Charlie and me down so it looks like we're out of control."

"Except Corinne helped that along on her own."

"Yeah." Tears slid down her cheeks, but she wasn't ready to crumble. Being honest fortified her. At least he knew the truth. "So yeah, that's my story. I am a princess who has run away from my problems and the rest of my life so I can start over. I want to move around without someone wanting something from me—photographs of me misbehaving, or naked, my attention to give money to their cause, to back their latest venture or just to see if I'm wearing something grubby. Then there are the guys who chase me."

"Who's been chasing you? What guy?" Luke asked. "Did you love that person?"

"I don't love Duke Elmore of Westland." She squared her shoulders. "He wants a virgin and a grander title. If he can snag me, then he thinks he's got a chance at being the king. He's nearly twenty years older than me, not attractive at all, and he's pushy." Her stomach quirked just thinking about the possibility she'd marry Elmore.

"He won't get a virgin now," Luke said. "He's too late."

Realization dawned on her. She'd lost her virginity to Luke and there was no way to get it back—not that she wanted to. She liked Luke and couldn't think of a better person to have experienced sex with for the first time. She'd known what she was doing, despite fearing her parents' wrath and had no regrets.

"He won't believe you, will he?"

"Not without checking." She shuddered. "You don't want to know how. It's barbaric and invasive." Her phone vibrated. She should check the device, but if she tried to answer a call right now, she'd crumble again. "You can look at it. I have nothing more to hide from you." She handed Luke the phone. "What's behind door number one?"

"Looks like you've got something from your social media accounts." Luke shrugged and offered the phone back to her. "I have a website for my art, but I'm still working out how to showcase my paintings on social media."

When she tapped the icon for her instant messages, photos of Corinne popped up with her name hash tagged. Another photo filled the screen, but this time it had #zaraorcatherine #newman #princess #mysteryman

She bowed her head. She'd grown used to the chase from the media, but Luke might not want to be pursued. Now she couldn't even have her middle name for cover. "Unfortunately, they've caught us together, so you're fodder for their intrusiveness."

"What in the hell?" He swiped through the images. "It's just us talking."

"Right, but we've gone viral." She pointed to the last image. "Everyone is trying to figure out who you are. They know where I am, but not your identity. We can keep it that way." She sighed. "If you want to stop seeing me, I understand. You don't need this kind of aggravation."

Instead of screaming, Luke laughed. "Viral. No shit. Who would've guessed?"

"I'm sorry." Everything was out of control. "It's not fair to you."

"Why are you sorry?" He tucked her hair behind her ear. "You don't need to apologize. I didn't know what I was getting into, but this isn't the worst thing that could happen to me."

"When the media finds out who you are, you won't be able to go anywhere. They'll follow you," she said. "They'll see your art and think you're doing something bad. You're not, but no one will believe me."

"Let them think what they will." He cupped her jaw. "You tried to tell me the truth before and I didn't get it. You came right out and said you were a princess."

"I did." She'd told him in a very half-assed manner, but still.

"Doesn't change how I feel."

"What doesn't?"

"You being a princess. It's not making me look at you in any other way. You're you. You're Zara, the sweet girl who got lost in the art building and asked for directions."

"You're sure?" He had to be joking. "This is bigger than you or me or a lot of things. It could bring you a whole hell of lot of attention you might not want."

"I'm positive." He traced the seam of her mouth with his index finger. "I knew there was something special about you from the start."

"You did?" Oh God. Was he going to use her being a royal against her now? Use her position to make money off the fact she'd posed for him? *Fuck...* "You figured out you can monetize our being together? If that's your plan, then you can just back up and I'll get out of your life. I left that behind and I'm not doing that for anyone, no matter how sexy he might be. I've had it with being used."

"Whoa." He laced his fingers with hers. "You're so wound up and you've been hurt a lot. I hate the people who screwed with you." He stared into her eyes. "I wasn't thinking anything about using you. What I meant is I knew you were special in that you have a light in you. There's passion and desire aching to come out. You're a vibrant woman who is figuring out her true worth. That's beautiful."

He'd shocked her. He'd seen everything she'd tried so hard to push to the surface. "Do you care that I'm a princess? I can't change your life. I suppose you could sell those pictures of me to the tabloids. They'd pay well--if that's what you want."

"You're perfect as you are, Zara," he said. "Any man who would ruin your trust isn't worthy of you. Besides, I don't want to be on that list of men who've let you down. You deserve better."

"Catherine," she corrected. "My first name is Catherine."

He crinkled his nose. "You strike me as a Zara. Catherine's too stuffy. You're a free spirit. Zara seems freer and sweeter, less controlled."

Less controlled. She liked the sound of that. "It's still new between us." She stared into his eyes. "I can't guarantee I won't be called home. My parents don't want me to be here at Kenton at all. Well, that's not true. My father probably doesn't care, but he's hard to read and my stepmother wanted me to stay in the castle to marry Elmore and have children. I don't remember my mother. She died when I was two."

"What about the video chat?" He frowned. "You've got a complicated life. Didn't you explain things to them?"

She wished she could explain things. "First, they didn't try the video chat. That was a fib from Corinne to get me to return to the apartment. I did hear from my parents, though. It was just the regular old phone kind of call and they weren't listening no matter what I said. This — me being here — is a silly thing in their mind. I'm wasting perfectly good time learning stuff when I could be reproducing. It's their principle."

He tipped his head and seemed to consider her words. "They'll rip you out of college, something you've worked for, on principle?"

"They will." The thought of losing her momentum made her stomach churn again. She sighed. "Once my father learns I'm not a virgin, my value will plummet.

He'll want to kill you because you were the one and will deem you unworthy."

"After he and the rest of them assassinate your character."

"You have to understand the dynamics of the family, but yeah. They're all about looks. It appears that the virginal, good-natured Catherine and we've brought her up well, so she'll make a proper wife. She'll abide your mandates without question and pop out those babies. If I marry another royal, then that gives us allies. The bloodline will stay pure-ish."

He rolled his eyes. "Then they'll doubly hate me when they see the pictures of you and my drawings," he said. "I haven't started more than the sketch for your painting, but the finished product won't help my case, will it?"

"Not a chance." She'd messed up her life in so many ways, but meeting and falling for Luke wasn't one of the ways. She wanted her freedom, but getting it risked her relationship with Luke.

"Hey." He held her hands. "You're an adult. You're consenting and the photos are tasteful."

"You don't understand." She trembled as fear rolled through her. "I got hung up on getting free from the family and I messed up. I should've thought things through and anticipated something like this would happen. I should've guessed Corinne would spill the beans."

"I think you did."

Her emotions got the better of her. "I don't want to be royal. I want to be me." She had no choice. It wasn't like she could stop being a princess. Abdicating wasn't a thing and she still wanted to spend time with her brother, Charlie.

He stared into her eyes for a long moment. "Are they coming for you? The guards or media or this Elmore?"

"I don't know." Fresh tears slid down her cheeks. She'd handled a lot, but couldn't handle any more today. "Damn it. I hate crying and I've done a lot lately. You must think I'm one gigantic crumbling mess."

"It's okay. This situation is crazy out of control. It's okay to fall apart with me." He tucked her to his chest. "You're going to stay with me for now. I don't know what Corinne was thinking, but she should've had your best interest at heart. She's not your sister, then, correct? You said she was something else."

"My lady-in-waiting."

"Ah. That makes more sense." He rubbed her back again. "I don't doubt your security team can keep you safe, but it'd give me peace of mind to know you're safe here. Okay? You need a space to be yourself and not have to think about putting on airs for anyone. I like you the way you are — messy, crumbly, sweet, sexy and human. I promise not to sell the pictures I take of you. Those are for my art. The only thing anyone will see is my series — with your approval to show it."

Even if she'd wanted to, she couldn't argue with him. He made sense and offered an out until the real shitstorm came.

"Will you stay with me?" he asked.

She sat up and wiped her cheeks again. "I will. We have a lot to learn together and you wanted to pose me. We should get going on those. I'm your girl and I want you to create art for me and of me."

His eyes lit up. "Yes."

Chapter Eight

Luke couldn't quite wrap his mind around everything she'd told him. The story seemed too fantastical. A princess? He'd seen her ID and her license. If the cards weren't real, they were great fakes, but he had the feeling they were legitimate. Why would someone fake being royalty? Not internet royalty, but actual? Besides, princesses were important figures, weren't they? He'd seen the social media posts. She had quite the following, but she didn't act like someone important. She came across so down-to-earth.

He still had a thousand questions for her, but he wasn't sure how to ask them. She'd been through a lot and the problems weren't over. Christ, the whole situation was messed up. How could a parent dismiss a child for wanting to find their way? How could someone not want their child to flourish?

"You're thinking too hard." She straddled his lap. "What's on your mind?"

"You're in trouble." He shrugged. "I guess I am, too, so it's a good thing we're in this together." He kissed her knuckles. "Should I be bowing to you or something? How am I supposed to act with a princess? Genuflect?"

"No." Her eyes widened a moment, then she smiled. "Please, don't genuflect. Be yourself—just like you are now. I like you being you."

"Then myself wants to shower with you." He patted her ass. "Last one in the shower goes down on the other."

She paused. "I've never done that. I've only ever seen videos. I'm not sure how to go down on you…"

"Then I guess you'd better beat me to the shower." He patted her bottom again. Damn, he couldn't wait to see her naked. The first time rocked him to his core. Now he'd have the chance to linger and explore her. Knowing she'd never had another lover piqued his interest, too. He could teach her, but they'd be learning together. How in the hell had he gotten so lucky?

She scooted off his lap and kicked out of her flats. "I hate to lose." She unzipped and shoved her shorts to the floor, then wriggled out of her panties. Her grin widened as she whipped her shirt over her head, then unhooked her bra. She shook out her hair. "Am I good enough?"

Fuck. She reminded him of a goddess. "Yes."

"I don't know how to go down on you," she murmured.

"I'll show you." He had precious little time with her and didn't want to squander it. He had no idea how long it'd be before the powers that be came to take her home. In the short time he'd spent with her, he'd seen her spirit and strength. He admired her determination.

She stepped into the stall first. Her hair darkened as she stepped under the spray. Droplets sparkled on her lashes and her skin glittered with water. She reached for him.

She stole his breath. He'd never seen a goddess outside of a painting, but she fit his description of one. He joined her in the stall.

"I've never showered with anyone before." She slid her palms over his chest. "Are you thinking I'm more trouble than I'm worth?"

"Nope." He lathered the washcloth. "Let me clean you. Turn around." When she did, he moved her hair off her shoulders. He soaped her back and along her neck, then down to the swell of her ass. Suds crept along the seam of her backside. As the water rinsed the bubbles away, he kissed the soft spot where her neck met her shoulder.

"Luke." She sighed. "I want to stay right here with you forever." She leaned into him. "It's not right, but I want it so much."

He knelt behind her and washed her legs. "Turn around to face me." He spied a dark mark on her leg. "You have a birthmark right below your bottom on your leg."

"I do. It's not my favorite thing, so I ignore having it." She wobbled, but did as told. Her hair splashed over her shoulders. When she smiled, she warmed his heart. "No one sees it because I'm worried the press will make a big deal. The last thing I need is for someone to make light of my imperfections more than they already do."

Luke worked his way up her body, washing and caressing her. He avoided her pussy and breasts until he cleaned the rest of her. He stood, then abandoned the cloth on the rack. He palmed her breasts and the soap slickened his way. He'd never get tired of touching her — so soft and perfect. He loved the feel of her breasts, heavy in his hands. She'd been made for him. Her nipples beaded. He leaned over enough to suck one into his mouth. Christ. She tasted like honey.

She jerked and moaned. "Luke." She slid her fingers into his hair. "Wow."

If she liked what he was doing now, then she'd love how he planned to touch her next. He eased one hand down her body to her belly, then to the apex of her thighs. He palmed her pussy, but didn't penetrate her. First, he wanted to give her time to adjust.

She held on to his head as he sucked on her breast. "Luke." She shivered.

Luke hummed against her chest, making her squirm. Water sluiced over her body. He eased one finger between her pussy lips, drawing a shudder from deep within her.

"Luke." She tugged on his hair and shuddered again. "I want to make you happy."

In a moment. He pinned her between his body and the wall. Water cascaded down on them as he knelt at her feet. He parted her cunt lips, baring the tender pink flesh. The scent of her arousal mixed with the soap and curled around in his brain. Cream coated her lips. He'd take more time once they were out of the shower, but he had to taste her right now.

She shivered again. "Luke." She ground on his face, bucking against him. "Feels so good."

That was what he wanted to hear. When she shivered again, he relented. So soft and smooth. He liked when his partner shaved. Plus, she intoxicated him. He licked his lips and stood.

She stared up at him, a dazed look in her eyes. "You stopped."

"Waiting makes later even better." He squirted shampoo onto his fingers, then worked the suds into her hair. She groaned and leaned into him again.

"I've never felt so cherished in my life." She reached around him and caressed his ribs. With her back to his chest, she situated his cock between her ass cheeks and rubbed him.

If she wasn't careful, he'd go off just from her touching him. He groaned. He hadn't been this close to the edge or this deep in so long. Maybe ever. "Rinse."

She let go and stepped under the spray. Suds and water curved along her body. She wiped her face, then glanced back at him.

"Fuck," he murmured. "I might be teasing you, but you're doing just as good a job of teasing me." He wanted to capture her between his body and the wall as he fucked her.

Her eyes flashed. "I'm trying to learn."

"You are." He grabbed the washcloth and added fresh soap.

"Let me." She took the cloth from him. "When I first saw you, a tingle shot through me." She smiled and smoothed the soap across his pecs. "All tanned and beautiful. I thought I'd been struck by lightning or zapped. I couldn't not look at you."

"You think I'm pretty?" *Christ.* He couldn't think straight. "That's not something anyone's ever said."

"I do." She moved to his abs, then groin. When she reached his erection, she abandoned the cloth in favor of her hands. "I've never done this before." She stroked him. "Tell me what to do."

"Go slow and light." He placed his hand over hers, guiding her up and down his shaft. "Like that." Soap slid down his body and added lubrication. He didn't feel the water, just her hands on him. Within moments, she picked up the technique of masturbating him and even managed to twist her hand. She toyed with his slit. The added sensation enhanced his pleasure. "Christ."

"Good?" She knelt between his feet and used both hands. "Yes?"

"Not so hard. Use one hand." He groaned, unable to think straight again. She was beautiful on her knees. Sinful.

She stroked his shaft, then flicked her tongue across the head of his dick. "Better?"

He tensed. *Oh God. So much better.* "Babe."

"I want to learn so I can make you happy." She resumed licking him. Water sluiced down her face. She reminded him of a water nymph.

Being with her made him happy and her mouth on him blew his mind. She parted her lips, welcoming him in.

Instead of pushing, he allowed her to set the pace. He palmed her head and planted his shoulders on the wall of the shower. "Yes, baby. Not so much teeth, but you're doing everything else right."

She glanced up at him and grinned.

The sight of his cock in her mouth, his princess taking care of him and showing him her devotion, knocked his senses inside out. She was so warm and inviting. When she sucked on him, she massaged his balls, too. For a novice, she learned quickly and excelled at the skills. He glanced down at her again and delight shimmered in his eyes.

The pleasure of her actions and the passion in her lovemaking overwhelmed him. He needed to feel her hands on him. *Fuck.* He wouldn't be able to hold back. Each time she bobbed her head, she pushed him closer to coming. He tensed, despite his best efforts to keep himself in check. *Nope, not going to happen.* He pumped his hips. She'd worked him into a frenzy.

"Zara." He eased away from her. "Fuck." He took over the act and stroked himself faster. His balls ached. "Give me your hand." His movements turned jerky as he continued to masturbate.

She rose on her knees and stroked him in time with his own ministrations. "Coming? Do it."

The tone of her voice, pleading, innocent and sexy, pushed him right over the edge. He jerked forward, but continued to rub himself. A thick ribbon of cum shot onto the shower floor. "Jesus."

She helped masturbate him until he stilled. "That's beautiful."

His knees weakened. He wobbled and helped her to her feet. Now that she'd relaxed him, he could focus on her now. He needed to. He rinsed, then cleaned her again. When she backed away from him, he twisted the knob to turn the water off. "Let me get a towel."

"I'm not going to break if I have to do something for myself." She stepped out of the shower first and grabbed the towel on the rack. "I'm not glass."

"I know." But knowing she was a princess changed things. He shouldn't see her any differently because she was the same person as before, but still. He took the towel from her and dried Zara, then himself. "But you are someone important. I don't want to unintentionally insult you by acting like a neanderthal or something."

"Luke?" She clasped her hands together, caging his between hers. "I'm sorry I lied to you." Her blush ran from her hairline to her chest. "I needed to know you cared before I could tell you the truth. You don't understand how it feels to not be loved for who you are. You also don't understand that there's nothing neanderthal you could do that would insult me."

He wanted to be upset with her, but had irritated himself. He couldn't change the fact she'd lied to him, but how could she know who to trust when everyone in her circles had ulterior motives? She wasn't upset with him for saying the wrong things.

"Do you know what made me trust you?" she asked.

"No." He followed her out to the main portion of the apartment. "Where is your brush? I'll detangle your hair."

"You like to brush hair?" She gave him the side-eye.

"Uh-huh. It's intimate and sweet, plus gives us time to recharge." He kissed the tip of her nose. "It's also sensual."

"Oh." She pulled the brush from her bag. "I...I trusted you because of your spirit. You didn't ask me about my past or my pedigree. You were nice and sweet when I needed help. Others would've expected something in return." She sank onto the bed. "It's what drew me to you."

He sat behind her and worked the brush through her hair. "I've never worked this hard for a relationship before."

"No?" She tensed. "Why?"

"Because I've never wanted anyone so much — no royalty involved." He ran the brush through her hair. "You make me happy. I want to do more than draw you. I want to learn every inch of you and taste you all over. I crave you."

She turned around and faced him. "Just remember that when they come for me."

"They will?"

"After seeing Corinne's behavior and my photos on social media, yeah. It's only a matter of time before someone comes looking for me."

"Then let's enjoy the hours or days we have." *Fuck.* He didn't want her to go. He had so much art to create and he'd fallen hard for her. He couldn't let his muse get away — not now and not ever.

Zara whimpered as he brushed her hair. Sure, he didn't have to take care of her, but she felt protected with him and special. He cared. No one else gave her such reverent attention. Her scalp tingled and she grinned to herself. Now that she'd been with him, she didn't mind being naked. Didn't mind him seeing her imperfections, either. Plus he was right. Having her hair brushed was one of the most sensual things she'd ever experienced.

She slid her hands over her body. Her nipples peaked and she moaned at the sensitivity. "Luke." He made her feel this way. The man had incredible power and she didn't want him to stop everything. Her life wouldn't be the same without him.

He pressed kisses to her shoulder and stopped brushing. "Yes, sweetheart?"

"I want to pose for you again." She placed his hand on her breast. "Now. Please?"

"Yeah?" He squeezed her breast, then rolled her nipple in his fingers. "I want you, too. Want you to pose for me, to stay in my bed, imprint yourself on me…"

"Yes." She ached into his touch. Her nerve endings were on fire. She rested her head on his shoulder. "Please?"

"You can, but in a little bit." He situated his hand between her legs. "I want to make you fly."

That was what she wanted, too.

"Stretch out on your back," he murmured. "We'll finish what we started in the shower."

It sounded like heaven to her. She scooted off his lap and scrambled onto the bed. What she lacked in experience, she'd make up for in enthusiasm. Tasting him and seeing him come thrilled her. She wanted to experience both again.

He parted her legs and passion shone in his eyes. He kissed along her leg to the inside of her knee. His moves were so tender that she whimpered.

She grasped the sheets and writhed. He hadn't even touched her pussy, but he already had her on edge.

His warm breath tickled her skin. The scent of his soap lingered on her skin. She grabbed the pillows to prop herself up to watch—she wanted to see everything.

He raked his teeth over her inner thigh, sending sizzles through her veins.

"Luke." She dug her toes into the bedding. She'd never felt anything so exciting in her life—except sex with him.

Without saying a word, he had her full attention. He parted her cunt and eased his tongue across her skin. The touch was so light, it could've been his breath instead. She wasn't sure.

She jerked toward him, needing more.

This time, he dragged his tongue across her sensitive skin, then feasted on her clit.

She moaned and threaded her fingers into his hair. The onslaught of sensations overwhelmed her. Her insides quivered. She bucked her hips, rubbing her pussy against his mouth. He sucked hard on the nub of her clit, eliciting a cry from within her. She had no idea how he knew what to touch to make her scream.

"More," she managed. "Oh God." She writhed. "Luke."

He continued to lick and nibble on her. Every so often, he hummed and the vibrations shot through her.

She tensed. A girl could only take so much, but she'd accept everything he gave her. She panted, but he managed to blow her mind again. He reached around her bent leg and palmed her breast. As she shuddered, he rolled her nipple between his thumb and forefinger.

The coil in her belly tightened. A fresh wave of excitement rolled through her veins. He kept giving her new things to experience. She moaned and words escaped her. She wanted to make noise and let him know she approved, but nothing like words formed.

He raked his teeth over her inner thigh again and continued to toy with her nipple. "Tell me you love this. Tell me."

"I do." She bucked against him. "Luke." He had her reduced to being able to say little more than his name. God, she couldn't think, just feel.

"Good girl."

His words vibrated down her spine. She shivered and the heat in her belly increased.

"Like that, babe. Let go." He resumed licking her pussy lips, then brushed his face in her cunt. At the same time, he speared one finger into her channel. He continued to tease her nipple.

She clamped down around him, needing to feel him surrounding her. He'd changed her. The coil wound tighter and she cried out. The combination of sensations on her body was too much to take. She rode his finger and pushed against his face.

Tingles filled her veins and warmth shot through her body. She trembled. The world seemed to melt away around her. Nothing else mattered except Luke and this moment.

She cried out again and the coil snapped. She tensed as the most overwhelming feeling washed over her. She swore she floated again. The room seemed to spin. She sagged against the bed and closed her eyes as she caught her breath. *Mind. Blown.*

He kissed her pussy once more, then withdrew his finger and let go of her breast. He stretched out beside her on the bed. She still couldn't think straight, but at least he was with her as she came down from the orgasmic high.

Luke tucked her to his side and petted her hair. "Beautiful."

"Yeah?" She'd call it sleepy or sated. She twined her legs with his. "Luke?" A hundred thoughts filled her mind.

"Sweetheart?"

"Did your series involve me being limp and happy? I can't remember," she murmured.

"Sort of." He traced the line of her jaw. "Do you want me to photograph you?"

"For the paintings." She snuggled closer to him. "I want the series to be everything you envisioned." Everything he could make it before they ran out of time.

"It will be." He pulled his phone off the side table. "Pose for me."

"Don't have to pose." She smiled. When he took the picture, she couldn't quite believe the woman in the image was her. She didn't resemble herself. The woman in the photo was happier, freer and in love. She smiled at the camera again. For the first time in her life, she'd made her own decisions, liked the direction in her life and wanted to keep this trajectory going.

He tapped the icon and took three more photos. Luke put the phone down, then turned over to face her. "You're irresistible."

"Because of my role?" God, she had to stop going right to that standard answer and trust him. "Tell me the truth."

"Because you're sweet and beautiful. You're open and caring, too." He switched off the light, then sighed. "We'll make a plan in the morning. If you've got any security people still loyal to you, we'll make sure you're safe so you can go to class. If not, then I'll do it alone."

"I can't go back to class. I've been outted." She clung to him. That part of her world, her college career, was over for now. "It's a matter of time before going to campus becomes a circus and no one in my classes will be able to concentrate. I'm a distraction because I'm a freak." She'd been through this before. "They'll ask me to go and say I'm welcome to stay on campus, but they'd like me to consider a lower profile."

He kissed her temple. "You're not a freak."

"Maybe not, but if I tell you we need to pull back or stay here, trust me. I know the score," she said. She'd been through this before when she tried to visit the art museum in Lysianna alone or when she'd tried to go shopping without her team around her. She'd been mobbed, then attacked. People wanted a piece of her. Maybe that wouldn't happen right away on campus, but eventually, someone would want something from her, a piece of clothing or a scrap of paper she'd touched, and they wouldn't quit until they got what they wanted.

"I trust you completely. I'll protect you and do whatever you want," he said. "You matter to me, Zara." He sighed. "I found my heart because of you."

She listened to the sound of his breathing. He'd fallen asleep. The sound was so rhythmic and soothing. Zara snuggled up to him and stared at the door. She had no idea how long she had until the royal guard showed up. They'd find her and her dream would end. How long would it be before she had to let Luke go? She didn't want to. Hell, she'd fight every step of the way—unless he couldn't handle the craziness of her life. Then she'd give him space. Still, she'd earned the right to have an education and a boyfriend who wasn't out to get his sticky hands on her title.

Right now, she had precious hours with Luke. She had moments with the guy who made her whole. She craved the life she'd created with him. Let the guards come. Let them try to take the prize she'd won. She'd fight. Her life mattered too much to give up. Luke mattered, too.

She'd found her heart in his hands. How could she ever walk away?

Easy. She wouldn't.

Chapter Nine

Zara woke to the smell of coffee. She blinked as she surfaced from sleep. Luke, clad in only a pair of jogging shorts, stood at the stove. A news program played on his tablet. She sat up and raked her fingers through her hair. Being with him and seeing him in the kitchen seemed so natural.

"You look like you belong in the kitchen," she said. "You're a man of many talents."

"I try." He glanced over his shoulder. "I made coffee if you'd like some, but I can make some hot cocoa or something else if you'd prefer. How did you sleep?"

"I slept well," she said. "I had the best snuggle bunny to keep me safe. I could get used to that every night."

"I could arrange that," he said and fiddled with a coffee cup.

"What time is it?" She looked for an alarm clock and found none.

"Seven-thirty." He brought the cup over and sat on the bed. "You don't want any, do you?"

"No, I'm good. I'll grab some cereal on campus or a granola bar." She folded her legs beneath her. Who was she kidding? She probably wasn't going to campus today. Her thoughts turned to Luke. "I've had a lot of firsts with you. Almost all of them, so yes, I should have some coffee or something to eat."

"It's time you lived." He grasped her hand. "Your phone's been going off for the last hour."

"My alarm?" Where was her phone? No, she hadn't set it. "It might be my social media. It's nothing big, I'm sure."

"No." He offered up the device. "Looks like texts and possibly a call. I didn't try to check it, but I noticed when the screen lit up."

"Thanks." She wasn't in the mood to deal with the shitstorm on the royal front. "I'm going to try calling Oren."

"Oren?"

"My guard. He's good at being out of sight, but right there when I need him. He used to be extra loyal to me." Until now. He could've been recalled by the king and could snatch her today to return her to Lysianna.

"What happens when they come for you?" He held the cup in both hands. "Do I have to bar the door?"

"I'm not sure. I've never run away before." She swiped through the notifications. One message caught her attention. Charlie. She brought up the text from her brother.

I admire what you've done. You need to live your life. Trying to hold them off, but no one listening. Oren is still guarding you, but Corinne has been discharged.

She dropped the phone. No more Corinne. *Fuck*. Her lady had screwed up on a colossal level. Zara rubbed her forehead. She should call her brother. Having to rely on others annoyed her, especially when she could handle things herself, but…Charlie held the power. She didn't.

She dialed her brother's number.

"Need privacy?" Luke asked.

She shook her head. "Stay." She waited three rings before Charlie answered.

"Catherine," Charlie said. "You're okay?"

"I'm fine. Why wouldn't I be?" She grasped Luke's hand. "Get me caught up. How is Shay? Or is there another guy in your life?"

"Shay is history," Charlie said. "He was like all the rest."

"He wanted to be queen?"

"And to get rich."

"I'm sorry." Her heart ached for her brother. He, of all people, understood her struggle.

"Forget him. You found someone and he's cute," Charlie said. "Proud of you."

"He is." She glanced over at Luke. "And he's not seeking anything."

"Good," Charlie said. "I tried to text you."

"I know." Their personal phones were monitored on all accounts, so she had nowhere to hide. "Lay it out for me. What do I need to know?"

"First, Corinne is out. Mother and Father don't believe she can be trusted after all those photos surfaced. They're on social media for anyone to see," Charlie said. "I agree she went too far, but she was supposed to be in Kenton to protect you, not have a party."

"She was lonely." She couldn't blame her lady for wanting to be normal, too.

"She might be and she has my sympathy. It's tough to be in our position because we live in a bubble and there's no way out," Charlie said. "I need to know she can be trusted, though."

"You do?" She noticed Luke leaving the bed and abandoning his cup. He picked up his camera. Did he want to photograph her on the phone? Interesting.

"I'll take over eventually," Charlie said. "I might as well start acting like a king and know what's going on."

"You should." She rubbed her forehead again. "What's the second thing?"

"Second, I talked with Oren. He's not leaving you. If Luke will work with him, then you'll be safe until the tornado arrives," Charlie said. "Don't bother going to class. It's all messed up and you're safer with your beau."

Tears pricked her eyes. She figured she wasn't supposed to leave, but hearing the words coming from Charlie cemented it in her mind. She should've known. "I'm done, huh?"

"Once Corinne posted the first photo, you were. She said she was you," Charlie said. "Guess even the ones closest to us can prove to be unworthy."

"Yeah," she said, her voice cracking. "What about the ones involving Luke and me?"

"Those are too grainy. You could've easily weathered those and I would've helped you," Charlie said. "I'd have given the media all sorts of false leads to keep them busy because you should be happy and if getting an education does it, then yeah."

"Thanks." She sighed. "Anything else?"

"Yeah. Mother and Father have sent envoys to retrieve you. No one knows where you are, so stay put. Shut your phone off. They won't grab you wherever you are if you're in a private building. It's only when you go to your apartment or out in public that they can grab you," Charlie said. "Stay in if you can."

"Already done."

"Smart girl," Charlie said. "But don't be surprised if Elmore shows up. He's spitting mad that you're not…as advertised any longer."

"As advertised?" Good God.

"A virgin."

"Oh." Yeah, she wasn't that any longer.

"Honey, you have to do what you have to do when it's right for you," Charlie said. "I won't judge and I will encourage you to be happy."

She spied Luke again. He'd put the camera down and instead held his sketchbook. He sat in the chair and seemed to focus on her. She sighed and turned her attention back to her brother. "So I'll assume I've been withdrawn from school."

"Mother started it yesterday," Charlie said. "The school wants the money, but not the publicity."

"It was bound to happen."

Charlie laughed. "You know, you could put a huge wrinkle in her plans."

"I could?" Why was he laughing?

"Yeah."

"How?"

"Get married."

"What?" She almost dropped the phone. "Charlie?"

"If Luke will do it, go to Vegas and get married. It'll stop Elmore in his tracks and will emancipate you from Mother and Father," Charlie said.

"What if he says no?"

"Even if it's annulled in twenty-four hours, you're free."

"And Luke?"

"Will he want something?" Charlie asked.

"I don't know if he'd go through with this, but if he does, he'll deserve something besides the honor of being..." She couldn't say husband. Luke wouldn't go along with the plan, even if it did make sense. He was a nice guy, but the relationship was too new to throw marriage into it.

"Tell him what you need and see what he says. If it's negative, then we'll figure out a plan B," Charlie said. "You could always marry Oren."

"Marry Oren?" He was older than Elmore and like a brother to her.

"Marry Oren?" Luke paled.

"I need to go," she said. "I've got to clean up this mess." She hung up on her brother and focused her attention on Luke. *Well, shit.*

Luke dropped his sketch pad. He'd drawn an image of her on the phone. The drawing reminded her of one of the suggested images for his series and evocative of deep emotion. Now she knew why he'd taken her photo.

"That's nice," she said. "For the series?"

"Yeah, sure." Luke frowned. "Who are you marrying? Oren? Since when?"

"I'm not marrying Oren." She explained the situation with Corine and Oren, then the issues with her going out into public. "See? I'm in over my head."

"They withdrew you from college? Without your consent?"

"My father is a king. He can do whatever he wants," she said. "If he threw money at the college, they just might bend to his will."

Luke laced his fingers together and propped his elbows on his knees. He rested his chin on his hands. "Elmore? Who is Elmore?"

"He's a duke who's on his way to find me." She couldn't lie to him any longer. "He's irked I'm not as advertised."

"Good. He doesn't deserve you." Luke picked up the sketch book. "If he can't see how wonderful you are, no matter what, then he's not worthy of you."

His words touched her. She deserved to be loved and cherished. "Do you?"

"Do I what?"

"Feel you're worthy of me?" She tugged the sheet around her body. "My brother gave us an out—if you want to take it."

"An out?" He narrowed his eyes and moved to the edge of the chair. "What out? What do you mean?"

"My brother will be king." She hated the tension between them. "He suggested something."

"Okay?" He frowned and his brow furrowed. "What's the out?"

"We get married." She held her breath.

"Fuck."

"No, we've already done that." She wanted to release the pressure, but how in the hell was that going to work when he seemed even more upset?

He snorted and the weight of the conversation seemed to evaporate. Luke shook his head. "Talk about rushing this."

"I know."

"It'd allow you to finish school."

"No, not right away. It'd get me out from under my parents' thumb, though."

Luke sagged in his seat. "Married? It doesn't seem right to push this." He shook his head. "You're being expected to do something out of honor, not love — even if it's me and who knows?"

She should've guessed he'd be hesitant. The situation was too much to spring on him. "It's just an option."

"It is." Luke left his seat and padded barefoot on the carpet, pacing the length of the room. "You should be your own person. You don't need a man to make you whole."

"Maybe." She agreed, but she did need to get married to get out from under her parents' rule.

"And you should make your own choices."

"Of course."

"You should select a husband out of love, not necessity."

"True."

He stopped pacing and stared at her. "It's just happening so fast. I'm gobsmacked."

"I know." She couldn't argue with him. "It was just a suggestion." One she rather liked. She could see them married and having a future. But he had to be convinced and that wasn't how she preferred to live her life. She tugged the sheet tighter around her body. Part of her wanted to go back to her apartment and stop making him feel so pressured. "I should get dressed."

"Zara." He sank onto the chair. "Babe."

"You're not ready for this, all of me and my issues. I get it." She kept the sheet around her torso. "I've imposed on you enough." Time to face her problems.

"Thanks." She started past him, but he caught her in his embrace. "Luke."

"Only a coward would back away when things get tough." He cupped her jaw. "I'm in way over my head, but I want this—us."

"You do?" She couldn't get her hopes up. Life kept kicking her ass every time she thought she could handle it on her own.

"I'm with you, princess. You're the most down-to-earth woman I've ever met. I don't know what to do, but I'm following your lead." He kissed her lightly on the lips.

She spotted a flash out of the corner of her eye. A flash? The last time she'd seen a... "Get down." She shoved Luke to the floor behind the bed. The coffee pot exploded. The sound of thunder echoed in the room as the mirror cracked and the window shattered. Glass flew all over the floor. Plaster chipped off the wall with the fourth and fifth booms. She hunkered down with him.

"What the hell?" Luke covered her with his body.

Little explosions continued around the room. With him practically on top of her, she scrambled into the bathroom. Her heart pounded. Someone was shooting at them. Someone wanted her dead.

"Hold still. You have glass in your hair." Luke slammed the bathroom door shut. "Those were shots, weren't they?" He paled. "Who?" His eyes widened. "Fuck. You're bleeding."

"Huh?" She stretched her leg and noticed the blood. "Must've been grazed. It's nothing. Are you okay?"

"Nothing? You could've been killed," Luke said, his voice cracking. "Where is that bodyguard of yours?"

"I don't know." She hunkered down with him. Fear gripped her, but she refused to show the emotion. "I'd like to know why I'm being shot at. Normally someone's trying to take my picture, not my life."

"Let me clean this up." He wetted a washcloth and placed it over the gash. "It's bloody, but you might be right and it's not bad. I think you were grazed."

"I'll be okay. I've been shot at before." She had to think this through. "Whoever covered your apartment in bullets knew we were here." She needed to check on Corinne and call the police after she alerted Oren. "Where...do you have a bandage? I can't wear a washcloth, especially when the police arrive."

"Just a moment." He produced a large square of gauze and tape from the cupboard.

Pounding echoed on the door. "Catherine? Princess?" The door burst open. Oren stood in the middle of the bathroom. "There you are. You're hurt."

"I'm fine." She held up both hands. "Did you call the police?"

"On the way. The team is trying to capture the shooter." Oren knelt next to her. "It came from the building across the common area." He smoothed the bandage over her leg.

"Luke saved my life." She allowed Luke and Oren to help her to her feet. "He's my hero."

"I know." Oren nodded to Luke. "Thank you. The crown should thank you, too. You've been brave."

Luke sank to the floor. "What's going on? You've been shot at before? Someone was aiming at us? What the hell!"

"My princess was targeted," Oren said. He tossed her clothes into the bathroom. "The crown offered a prize to the person who could deliver her home.

They're out for blood." He fiddled with his phone. "The police are on the way up, so get dressed."

"The person...they're trying to kill her," Luke managed. He shook his head. "We need to keep her safe."

"It's too late. Forces for the crown are here." Oren closed the door. "Get dressed, my princess. The team is here to take you home."

The lump in her belly grew and she wobbled into her clothes. Her parents had sent a team to bring her home. *Wonderful.* The police would be there and see the mess. They'd wonder why she was in the States without much protection. The college would never ask her back and Luke...God. What did he think? She dressed in silence and prayed Luke wouldn't decide to walk away.

"They can't take you," Luke said. "It's not right. You have a life here. You're learning and spreading your wings."

She settled on his lap and draped her arms around his neck. "I never thought I'd find someone like you. I didn't think it was possible to be loved for myself and you've proven it's possible."

"Zara." Pain shimmered in his eyes. "We're not done, babe."

"No, we're not."

"But you have to go." He held tight to her. "I can't come with you, can I?"

"Not yet." Heaviness filled her mind. She hated leaving him. When she left the bathroom, the cops had arrived. She reached into her bag and handed the rabbit to Luke. "This is my most prized possession. I know it and you will find your way back to me. I can't sleep without it or you."

"Princess?" Oren opened the door. "Time to go before there's a scene. You can give your statement in the corridor." He held out his hand.

She placed her college ID in Luke's palm. "I don't know how or when, but I *will* find you."

Three men in black jackets with gold piping stood in the corridor. The police taped off the room and herded Luke over to the bathroom. Zara reached for Luke as the jacketed men spirited her away from the man she loved. Tears slipped down her cheeks. This wasn't the end of her story with Luke. No way.

She stole one last glance at him and her life as she knew it. No matter what she had to do, she'd come back to Luke.

Had to.

Chapter Ten

Luke stared at the empty space where she'd been. *Gone.* He answered the cops' questions and gave his statement. Police officers took samples and prints. Glass spread across the floor. Christ, he had a huge mess to clean up. He stepped on a shard. At least he hadn't cut his foot. No one seemed to be interested in helping him pick up the pieces.

He held on to the rabbit and Zara's ID. The items were the only traces of her he had, save for his drawings. His heart ached. Jenna had left him because she claimed he loved art more than her. Things weren't the same with Zara.

Do I love Zara?

Sure feels like it.

He hugged the rabbit. She said she'd come back. He should've given in to her idea and married her. He couldn't imagine his life without her. Would they have had time to get to Vegas? He'd never know.

Another man with a black coat and the gold piping moved him from the room and into the hallway. Corinne waited outside his door.

"You've got a mess," she said. "She was shot at, wasn't she?"

"Yeah." He tamped down his irritation. She'd helped cause the problems for Zara. "You had a good gig. Hang out with her and protect her."

"You don't understand. I was lonely. I get to see her with the beautiful people and I know she hated that life, but I wanted to try it."

"You helped ruin her life."

"I know." She folded her arms. "I'd blame my problems on the rum, but we both know better."

"Yeah, well, now she's gone." He rubbed the ID against his thigh and squeezed the rabbit in his other hand. "I have shit to do and can't because my room is a crime scene."

"I know." Corinne bowed her head. "I'm here to offer you the apartment I shared with Zara. Her stuff is there and the security staff is continuing to protect it."

"What about my stuff? My life?" He still had his sketches and electronics to retrieve. He could replace his stuff, but he couldn't replace the art.

"We'll move it upstairs," Corinne said. "I might not work for the crown any longer and I might have destroyed her trust in me, but I know you two belong together. I want to help you get back to her."

"Right." He pressed the rabbit to his face and breathed in Zara's scent. "I'd like to clean up my place so I can figure out what to do next." He growled. "Fuck. I'm going to be on the hook for the damage. I can't afford this." Plus, he needed to pay somehow for a plane ticket to Lysianna. He needed a passport, too. Christ, there were too many rules.

Corinne placed her hand on his chest. "I talked to Charlie."

"Who?" He tucked Zara's ID in his shorts pocket. "What?" He shook his head again. "I need to get dressed and I can't even get to my clothes."

The man with the jacket snapped his fingers. Corinne nodded and directed Luke down the hallway.

"We've got a change of clothes for you in our apartment." Corinne stood beside him in the elevator. "Charlie is Catherine's brother. He believes you and Catherine are a match."

"Great." He followed her to the apartment she'd shared with Zara. "So what?"

"He's on your side," she said. "Do you have faith you belong with Catherine?"

"Zara," he said, correcting her as she handed him a pile of folded clothes.

"Yes. Do you?"

"Yes." He ducked into the bathroom. He needed to check on his canvases and protect the art from anyone wanting to filch it. He dressed in moments, then left the bathroom. "Now what? I've got shit to retrieve."

"Luke, stop." Corinne touched his arm. "Charlie is going to help you."

"He is?" He tamped down his aggravation. "Why should I believe you?"

"You shouldn't. I screwed up and I'm paying for it, but I'm also heading to Lysianna," Corinne said.

"How?" He stared at her. Nothing made sense.

A guy who looked a lot like the male version of Zara, except taller and thinner, strolled into the living room. He had the same shade of dark blond hair and dark eyes. A half-smile curled on his lips. "You must be Luke."

Good thing he'd gotten dressed. "Do I know you?"

"I'm Charlie, Zara's brother." He gestured to the four men with him. The guys, sans gold piping, reminded Luke of secret service folks. Charlie notched his chin. "I want that apartment cleaned up and everything belonging to Luke brought up here to this apartment. Now."

Luke stood next to the sofa. He should be irritated at Charlie taking control, but honestly, he needed someone to handle the madness. Charlie was Zara's brother. Maybe he'd have her best interests at heart. "Why are you doing this?"

When the men left, Charlie closed the apartment door and gestured to Luke. Corinne exited without a word. Once she was out of the room, Charlie spoke. "They'll move your stuff up here where it's safe. I don't want you to be exposed." He dipped his head. "I saw your art and I'm impressed. I'll admit I don't want to see my baby sister in such a manner, but I know how she feels about you. If she trusted you enough to be that vulnerable, then you're special to her."

"She's special to me." He tensed as the first guy brought back Luke's camera and phone. Luke nodded to show appreciation and tucked the phone into his pocket. Her brother didn't need to see the photos he'd taken—not all of them. "Whose clothes are these? The ones I'm wearing?"

"Mine." Charlie grinned. "You're about my size and those aren't covered in blood or glass."

"Thanks."

"Now, the problem is, you're being watched and could be attacked," Charlie said.

"What about you?" Wasn't Charlie exposed, too?

Charlie laughed. "Like my sister, I wanted to get out and experience the world. I've got a man at the palace who looks enough like me to give me the chance to get away. My folks think I'm there."

"What about Zara?"

"All in good time." Charlie nodded to the bed. More men brought in Luke's art and his computer. Once they left again, Charlie sighed. "I see she left you the rabbit. It's so like her. She's innocent in a lot of ways."

"It's silly, I suppose, for her to leave it, but she said she'd find her way to me," Luke said. He fingered the soft fabric of the rabbit, happy to have something of hers so close.

The men returned to the apartment with Luke's safe, his books, personal belongings and clothes. The art and photos from the wall ended up in a pile on the table. His art supplies were stacked in Zara's former bedroom. Even the rangy potted plant was brought to the apartment.

Corinne returned to the living room and Charlie left his seat. He paced the length of the room. Luke wanted to do something, but what?

"Do you have everything?" Charlie asked. "Is it clear?"

"Yes, my prince." The first man bowed. "Clean, save for the furniture already belonging in the apartment." The group of men left again.

"They're doing one more sweep," Charlie said. "It's being handled."

"Is it?" Luke held tight to the rabbit. "So, I'm here. Am I safe?"

"You are now." Charlie dismissed Corinne again and she left the apartment. "She's not a threat. Just a woman who made the wrong choice on account of rum."

"It happens." He stayed on the sofa. He wasn't sure he trusted Charlie or anyone.

"First, people within the kingdom knew about Catherine coming here," Charlie said.

"Zara." He preferred calling her by that name.

"Right." Charlie smiled. "She always seemed like more of a Zara than Catherine to me, too. But back to the point. People knew she was coming her. Advisors encouraged us to branch out and get experience. What some failed to realize is that she's the only one of us who can produce an heir. I could, but not with my future partner."

"Because you're gay? You could have a surrogate." Luke shrugged. "It's done."

"I could, but the crown won't accept the person producing the egg is good enough. The advisors who wanted me to get experience would claim the woman and child aren't worthy." Charlie held up both hands. "It's a mess."

"Then I guess it's no different than if Zara and I had children." The very idea of having a family with Zara blew his mind. He wanted children eventually and could see her as a mother. She'd be great. But so soon? What if she didn't want kids?

"True. Zara is the one who can produce heirs, though," Charlie said. "She's supposed to be in a relationship approved by the crown — at least one that's been approved by the time her portrait is revealed." He shook his head. "My position in the kingdom isn't important right now — keeping my sister from having a shitty fate is. There are people around her that don't want what's best for her."

"Corinne?"

"No. She just made a bad choice." Charlie waved his hand. "I mean the others. The second issue is those others. Did she or Corinne mention Elmore?"

"The duke? Yeah, they both said he's gross, older and not the one Zara likes," Luke said.

"That's him." Charlie smiled. "I didn't think he'd won her over."

"No."

"Our parents tried to push certain people in our direction to encourage a match. Our parents aren't a love match, but rather a strategic one," Charlie said. "It shows."

"They sound miserable."

"You could say that." Charlie sat on the arm of the chair. "They didn't choose each other and don't believe a thing."

"Of course."

"Baby girl believes in love and romance," Charlie said. "Elmore's not in love with her, but with the crown."

"He's probably kissing up to an advisor, trying to get someone to convince Zara to marry him," Luke muttered. "He wants her for his own reasons and it's not love."

"Bingo."

Luke stared at Charlie. "You're joking. He'd do that to her? For a title? Money?"

"Both."

"Fuck."

"Elmore wanted her to fall for him because he's older and has money. She wasn't impressed with his title or that money. She saw right through his power grab."

"Plus, she didn't like him." Luke settled back in his seat. "He's not the happy ending she deserves."

"Correct." Charlie nodded. "We can't be sure and the police are helping with the investigation, but it's assumed Elmore was behind the shooting."

"Why?"

"To scare you and Zara. To make her think she's in danger when she's with you." Charlie shrugged. "It didn't work."

"She was shot. Whoever did the shooting grazed her." Luke tensed and he bounced his foot. He couldn't shake the edginess. "I want to see her. I want out of here and to go to her. She's my heart."

"I knew that from the moment I saw you." Charlie clapped his hands. "I'm not happy she was hurt, but I'm forever grateful you protected her."

"What are you going to do about her getting hurt?" Luke asked. "I'd give my life to keep her safe."

"I'll do everything in my power to capture the bastard who did it and have him go before the crown. He won't get away with it." Charlie sighed. "But I knew you'd do that. I needed to hear it, but I had the feeling. I do have a question. Why did you have her pose in such a vulnerable manner?"

"For an art project." The images had been for a project. For all he knew, his college career was over. "She volunteered to model for me."

"She's always had an adventurous streak," Charlie said and held up one of Luke's drawings, the one of Zara on the balcony. "This one speaks to me. It says she's lonely and broken, but still has her spirit."

"Exactly."

Charlie turned his attention back to Luke. "I would like you both to be able to finish your respective degrees. You've worked too hard to be stalled now."

"But?"

Charlie smiled. "You're smart. You can see the endgame. She won't be able to return to college until Elmore is in custody. No one is safe here—not even you. So...I'd like you to become my personal artist on the palace grounds."

Luke stared at her brother. "Wait. What?" Charlie had to be joking.

"I need a personal artist. One who understands the nuances of the subject, can evoke motion and happens to be in love with my sister," Charlie said. "Sounds like you."

The wind rushed out of Luke. He knew to his core that he loved Zara, but hearing the Charlie vocalize Luke's thoughts was almost too much to take.

"You do, don't you?"

"I do."

"Good."

"She wanted me to marry her," Luke whispered.

"And you hesitated."

"I didn't want her to be tied down to me if she thought I wasn't worthy. I don't want her to do something that isn't right for her." He couldn't see his life or future without Zara in it, but he refused to force her.

"Luke, I can't get you married to her now," Charlie said. "She's going home to the court where our parents will give her the tongue-lashing of her life. She might even be barred from leaving the castle grounds." He leveled his gaze at Luke. "If you love her in the way I think you do, then prove it."

He gripped the arm of the sofa and pieced through what Charlie had said. Luke had a chance to be with Zara again.

"I can't guarantee you'll get to see her right away. They'll probably have her under lock and key for a while, but you can establish yourself at court and do art," Charlie said.

"And when the family sees my art?"

"They'll want to string you up." Charlie folded his arms. "So what? You've never faced issues for your art?"

"I have."

"Then don't sweat it." Charlie crossed his legs. "I've taken care of this apartment and the one you occupied. There will be no charges against you and our court will deal with the police now that you've given your statement. The royal police have taken Zara home and recorded her statement, too."

"Shit. Talk about efficient." Luke toyed with the ear of the rabbit. "I guess you'll get your man."

"I wish," Charlie said. "Oh well. About Corinne. She'll be sent back to Lysianna and dealt with there. The job of court artist is open and if you work with me, you'll get what you want."

Luke nodded. "Let me contact my professors. I'll try to get them to let me do my work remotely."

"Call this an internship." Charlie shrugged and uncrossed his body. "I'm leaving at one this afternoon. Get yourself in order and we'll go."

"How are you able to get all of these things done with such speed?" Luke asked.

"I'm a prince." Charlie grinned. "I'm a prince, I love my baby sister, I want one of us to be happy and I'm tired of my people being walked on. If this helps one of us, then it's a win."

Luke couldn't argue with the logic, especially if he could be back with Zara. "Let's do this thing."

* * * *

Four hours and a brand-new passport later, Luke sat on a private jet streaking across the sky. The plane wasn't huge, but large enough and bigger than Luke would've expected. Rich wood covered many of the surfaces while plush carpet cushioned his footsteps and screamed luxury. He'd never been in a private jet before, just a packed flight from Ohio to Colorado once.

Corinne sat across the aisle and alternated between quiet crying and tearing up a tissue. He wanted to help her, but wasn't sure how. Why should she be pushed out of her job for one mistake? Zara was being held accountable for her actions, but still. Everyone needed a goof up from time to time.

Luke leaned over and touched Corinne's arm. "Hey."

"Hi," she said, her voice soft. She stared out of the window instead of at him.

"Are you looking forward to going home?" Luke asked.

"No." She balled her tissue. "I worked for the court and had standing. Now, I have nothing. My parents won't allow me home because I've disgraced the family — and myself."

"It's not all that bad." The situation looked bleak, but things could be worse. "This is your chance to be your own person, too."

"You don't understand. I had a job and a place to live." She faced him. Her makeup had smeared and the circles under her eyes darkened. "It wasn't great work and I complained, but I was secure. I had a good friend in Zara."

"You still do."

She rolled her eyes. "You're so young."

"How old are you?"

"Twenty-three."

A year older than him. Not ancient. "You've got your whole life ahead of you."

"I lost my best friend."

"Zara isn't as angry with you as you think."

"Right," she snapped. "How do you know?"

"Because when we got shot at, she made sure I was okay, Oren was called, then worried about you. Yes, she walked out of the apartment, but she doesn't hate you," Luke said. "It was odd to go by her name, but I get it. You wanted a taste of her life."

"I did." She averted her gaze. "I also hoped Charlie would notice me."

"He's gay."

"I know." She wasn't crying any longer, but seemed more defeated. "He'll never want me, but if I pretended to be Zara, I could pretend to be close to him."

"Because he's going to be important?" No wonder the family had trust issues.

"No." She offered a half-smile. "He's my only crush. That guy at the party…he was just an experiment. He thought I was pretty enough, I guess, and I thought if he could find me attractive, why not Charlie? You know?"

"There's someone out there for you. He won't care if you're on the court or if you're a working girl. He'll see the beauty inside you and the sizzle will overwhelm you." He felt that way about Zara.

"Is that what happened with Zara? So fast?"

"It is." He fiddled with his watch. He'd been given the timepiece when he graduated high school. He'd never have anything fancy or money to take care of Zara properly, but he could offer his heart — worn and battered like the watch. "I'm not good enough for her. I'm poor, my folks are dead, I'm an artist and I get too wrapped up in my art. I'd just as happily spend my money on paint and canvas as I would food." He chuckled. "I had an ex-model tell me once I told Zara the truth and she saw my involvement in my art, she'd leave. I didn't date my models until I met Zara. I also didn't believe in love, then she came along."

"You don't believe in love?"

"I didn't until I met her." He focused on Corinne. "She came into my life and I didn't think twice."

"She does love you."

"And someone out there is just waiting to fall in love with you." He patted her arm. "Give yourself a chance."

"I will."

"What do you like to do? Art or writing or anything?"

She blushed. "No one has ever asked me."

"I am."

"I liked taking care of Zara. We talked about guys and clothes, but I love to sing. I used to sing while I cleaned her quarters." She stopped playing with the tissue. "I like makeup, too. I used to do Zara's when she went on official outings."

He wasn't sure how much he could help her, but he had an idea. "What if I put in a good word for you with

Charlie and Zara, and got you in doing her makeup? It wouldn't be as inclusive as before, but you'd get to see Zara and you'd have time to have a life, too."

Her eyes watered. "You'd do that? Why?"

"You made a mistake and admitted it. One stumble doesn't make you a bad person and doesn't mean you can't grow. You should be happy and if that means helping Zara and growing separate from her, then you should."

"Thank you." She left her seat and hugged him. "Now I know why she loves you. You really are a good person."

"And she loves you." He winked, then settled in his own seat.

Charlie strode past Luke and gestured to him, signaling him to head to the rear of the plane. When Luke joined him, Charlie held up his glass.

"Kudos, old man." Charlie sipped the amber drink. "You just might have a future as an ambassador."

"Huh? I'm an artist." He leaned against the wall. "What are you talking about?"

"You defused the situation with her. Smart man."

"I might have promised her something that's impossible."

"I heard," Charlie said.

"And?" Luke held his breath. He could be in big trouble.

"Unless Zara has a problem with it, Corinne being her makeup artist is a good choice. It's still a job and she'll be with Zara, but she'll have freedom, too. It's the best of both worlds and a good answer for the problem." Charlie nodded. "Plus, it gives you another in to see Zara."

"I won't be able to see her, will I?" *Fuck.* The only reason he'd agreed to be the court artist was to be with the woman he loved.

"She'll get you in for personal reasons." Charlie waggled his eyebrows. "I can only get you in to take Zara's portrait." He sipped his drink. "But if my sister happens to escape her confinement and goes with you to another portion of the castle, I won't argue."

Although his hope rose, Luke understood. He was up against some strong forces wanting to keep him apart from Zara. But he could change the outcome. He could get his way and had allies to do so.

"How about you focus on being the best court artist I could hire?" Charlie grinned, then ducked into the room at the back of the plane.

Luke shrugged. Charlie's idea sounded like a good idea to him. He'd go to Lysianna, paint her portrait and prove to Zara he loved her.

Easier said than done, but he trusted his heart and Zara.

Chapter Eleven

Zara stared at the ceiling in her bedroom. She'd become a prisoner. She'd been back from Kenton for three days and not allowed to leave her quarters for any reason. Not for a stretch, fresh air...nothing. She could still hear her stepmother's words on a loop in her mind. *'You let us down. You acted like a commoner and misbehaved. Princesses don't act out. Until you can accept your role, you will stay in the castle.'*

Until she could accept her role... More like until she admitted she'd been bad and wouldn't do it again. Then she wouldn't be a captive.

She squeezed her eyes shut. Three days since she'd left college and three days since she'd seen Luke—they'd been the longest of her life. In only a few weeks on her own, she'd found her heart. She couldn't expect Luke to come for her. He'd probably be barred from Lysianna.

A knock at her door interrupted her thoughts. She opened her eyes. "Go away." She wasn't in the mood to be insulted again. "No admittance."

The knob moved and door opened. Charlie ventured into her quarters. "You'd kick me out?"

She lunged off the bed at her brother and bear-hugged him. "I missed you."

"Missed you, too, kid." He hugged her tight. "How was college?"

"You already know." She released him. "You've already graduated."

"Yeah." He shrugged. "How is Luke?"

"I don't know. I haven't contacted him. Call it shame or embarrassment, but I don't know what to say to him. It was so crazy...he might not want to talk to me." She sank onto the bed. "Think you can get me out of here? I want to go somewhere."

"You will," he said. "How's the leg?"

"Healed for the most part. It doesn't bother me." She'd tried to forget the shooting. "I might be dead if it weren't for Luke."

"You might be dead because you were with him," Charlie said. "That's why you were targeted—you were with someone else."

"Who shot me? Elmore? Someone from the crown?"

"I'm still working on that. In the meantime..." He snapped his fingers. "I would like you to meet your new makeup artist. It's a probationary position, but I think it'll work into something permanent."

"Huh? Probationary?"

Corinne stepped into the room. "Hi."

Charlie nodded. "Probationary and conditional on your wishes. If you'd like a makeup artist, then she's yours. If not, then the deal I made with her is a no-go."

"Deal? Charlie?" Zara shook her head. Corinne was there and she couldn't believe her eyes. "I don't know what to say."

"I'll be right back." Charlie ducked out of the room, leaving her alone with Corinne.

Her former lady-in-waiting held up a makeup case. "Shall we get to work?"

"I..." She wasn't sure how to feel. Corinne was still her best and only friend. How could she kick her out? She couldn't.

"I'm here to do your makeup." Corinne opened her case. "I'm supposed to make you beautiful for your official portrait."

"Huh?" She didn't know a thing about this portrait. "Hold on. Corinne? How did you get in here?"

"If you don't want my services, then say so."

"I want a second to understand." She stilled Corinne's hands. "You're here."

"I am."

"Are you okay?"

"I miss my best friend and I can't stop feeling guilty about what I did because I ruined your trust," Corinne said. "So no, I'm not okay, but I'll deal."

Zara grasped Corinne's hand. "Come here. You didn't ruin my trust."

"That's what Luke said, but I'm scared."

"Luke? You spoke to him?" Zara asked. "How is he?"

"He's good," Corinne said. "He gave me a pep talk."

"Oh. Are you with him?" God, she hoped not. She couldn't handle being tossed aside that fast.

"No, but I did meet someone." Corinne smiled.

"The guy at the party?"

"No. His name is Ari. He's a pilot."

"Wow." A pilot? Good job. "I'm proud of you." She missed this closeness. Things were different between her and Corinne, but a lot was still the same. "You're my makeup artist?"

"Luke suggested it and Charlie approved the role, as long as you're okay with it."

"I've had my lady taken away from me." She hated being lonely and sounding sad. She'd tired of the distance between her and her friend. "Please stay. It gives us the chance to talk." Maybe she'd get more information on Luke, too. "I forgive you, but you always had my forgiveness."

"Thank you." Corinne hugged Zara. "Now, it's time to get you ready."

"For the portrait?"

"Yes." The light sparkled in Corinne's eyes. "It'll be a long sitting. We need to make you beautiful and worthy of an official portrait. Ready?"

"You've got your work cut out for you with me. I'm not beautiful."

"Right." Corinne abandoned her case. "You shower and I'll pick out the dresses. Then we'll get your hair in order. I have the list for what's required."

"What?" She stayed put on the bed. "Requirements? This was my stepmother's idea, wasn't it?"

"Before you get upset, no, it wasn't your stepmother. These are Charlie's suggestions."

"Oh." She allowed Corinne to nudge her to the bedroom. "Then you're allowed to stay?"

"For this anyway." Corinne shoved her into the bathroom. "We have a deadline, so don't goof off."

No use in arguing. She stripped and turned on the water, then stepped into the shower. Getting clean wasn't as much fun without Luke to share the space.

She washed her hair and body, but with each swipe of the cloth, she missed Luke's touch and the sound of his voice in her ear. She could almost hear him and the memory sent shivers down her spine. Heat engulfed her and she swore she felt his hands on her body. She sighed. There was no point in worrying about Luke and the past right now. One way or another, she'd find her way to Luke. Soon. She just had to formulate her plan.

She left the shower and dried off in the bedroom. Corinne fiddle with two ballgowns — one black and one navy blue. Zara hadn't worn either gown in over a year. She fingered the navy silk.

"Isn't this one rather sexy for an official portrait?" Zara asked. "It's provocative."

"Charlie said the blue would look perfect against your skin. The color isn't as severe as the black, so I'm leaning toward the blue." Corinne pointed to the chair. "Sit. I need to get you ready."

"Sure." She did as told. Corinne impressed her with the dexterity she used to dry and style Zara's hair. Zara hated trying to do her own hair and never had mastered makeup. Within an hour, her makeup was done, her hair in place and jewelry chosen. Corinne helped squeeze her into the corset, undergarments then the gown.

"Okay, stand." Corinne backed up. "Put the shoes on and twirl." She folded her arms. "It'll do."

"I hope so." She couldn't breathe without the corset threatening to bust her chest free. The neckline revealed plenty of her cleavage. Maybe she should change into something more demure.

Corinne tugged the shoulders of the dress down, increasing the view of her bust. "There we go."

"Charlie requested this?" She picked up her phone and took a selfie. "I want to send a picture to Luke."

Corinne nodded. "You look like a real queen."

"Thanks." She stepped into her pumps. "Where to?"

Before she vacated her suite, the door opened and Duke Elmore rushed into her room.

Zara sucked in a ragged breath. She didn't want him to get the wrong idea. "Elmore."

"My princess." He kissed her hand. "You look lovely. Almost like you're expecting me. I might suggest you wear red next time."

"I see." There wouldn't be a next time.

"Your college beau hasn't followed you," Elmore said. "He couldn't come along, I expect? He won't be trying."

She gritted her teeth. "Get on with your point." She slid her gaze over him. He might only be forty, but he seemed ancient. He wasn't in the age range she preferred—closer to hers. Tall, with blond hair and green eyes, he might be attractive to someone else. He seemed to wear a permanent frown and be leering at her. Not attractive. He also wasn't getting the hint she wasn't interested.

"Your brother won't be providing an heir," Elmore said. "It falls to you to do that."

"It does." Not that she'd be asking him to help her produce said heir.

"You need a suitable husband to help you create the next king." Elmore smiled and reached for her hand. "My beloved."

"I'm not your beloved." She yanked her hand away. "I'm also late."

"Late?" Elmore asked. "For?"

"An engagement," Corinne said. "You need to go."

"I'm told you're no longer her lady and have no standing here," he said. "So shut up."

"Don't talk to my lady that way." Zara wiped her hands on her dress. "Excuse me."

"Before you go, consider my offer. You need to marry someone not only worthy of you, but who can love you properly," Elmore said. "Marry me."

"No. I'm not marrying anyone any time soon." She shook her head. "Excuse me."

"Just a moment." He withdrew a bracelet from his pocket and snapped it around her wrist. The jewelry caught the light and the red stones shimmered. "Consider these jewels pretties for my perfect jewel."

"You should keep this." She tried to unhook the clasp. "I can't accept it."

"Too late." He kissed her cheek. "Consider my offer. We belong together." He dipped his head, then left. He moved as quietly as he had when he'd arrived.

She sagged into Corinne. "He won't quit."

"Nope." Corinne removed the bracelet. "I'll put this on your makeup table. Shame, really. It's a pretty bracelet, but he's an ugly-spirited man." She sighed. "You do realize he thinks you're going to marry him."

"I said no."

"But your parents will say yes."

Zara lowered her voice. "I'm not a virgin any longer."

"I suspected as much." Corinne smiled. "Luke?"

She nodded.

"Good. He loves you."

"He's in the States. I'm here." Her voice caught. "Love doesn't mean much with the distance between us." *Distance, laws, rules…*

"I know."

She refused to marry Elmore. She'd rather live alone than be tied to a man she detested. "We should go. Where are we heading? I missed the location."

"I didn't get to tell you because we were interrupted. We're going to Charlie's sitting room. This way." Corinne opened the door for her and escorted her across the corridor to Charlie's group of rooms.

Zara blinked. The severe lighting in the suite made seeing where she was going almost impossible. A single lounge chair waited in front of a black cloth drape. Charlie stepped out of the shadows.

"Hi, you." He hugged her. "Hi, Corinne."

"My prince." Corinne retreated. "We're ready."

Charlie snapped his fingers. "We have a new court photographer. He's going to take your official portrait. Sit here." He gestured to the velvet chaise lounge. "Just a moment."

She settled on the chaise as Corinne arranged the folds of the dress. When Corinne backed up, Charlie returned and waved to the photographer.

"I'd like you to meet Luke Cobb," Charlie said. "Our newest photog."

"Luke?" The moment she saw him, her heart skipped a beat. "It's you!"

"I'm sorry. That's right. You need full privacy while taking the photographs," Charlie said. "Corinne? We should go and leave the artist to his work. We'll be right back." He and Corinne exited, leaving her alone with Luke.

Zara blinked, then turned her attention to Luke. He hadn't said a word. She wished she understood what was happening. Still, Luke had a camera and stood before her.

"You're here." She fought the urge to throw herself into his embrace. "Are we truly alone?"

"We are," Luke said. "Charlie worked it out. I do have to take your photograph. I was hired for the job."

"You were?"

"Well, yeah. I'm really here as the court photographer. Eventually, I should have to take everyone's photo." He knelt in front of her and placed the camera on the floor. "He invited me to do this job so I could see you. My heart broke when you left."

"Mine, too." She smoothed the wrinkles in his dress shirt. In casual or fancier wear, he mesmerized her. She ran her fingers through his hair. "What do we do? I don't want you to photograph me. I'd rather kiss you."

"In case we're interrupted, let me arrange you and get these pictures taken. Once that's done, we'll talk." He stood and moved the lights, focusing on her face. "Turn so you're looking over your shoulder. Lean on the chaise. I'll tell you where to focus."

When she did as told, he moved her necklace and freed a curl from the pins in her hair. He stood off to the side of the camera. "I want you to look over here and like you can't wait to get me alone."

"I can't wait to get you alone." She added a slight smile, trying to be coy. She loved this man and needed time with him, but how to make that happen?

He ducked behind the tripod. "Good."

She held still. "I'd rather do the photos like the ones you took in Kenton."

"We will." Luke stepped out from behind the camera. "Smile a little more. Just a little and keep it light."

She watched him and did as he'd asked. Hunger spiraled through her veins and not for food. She wanted him. She'd rather be out of the dress and corset in favor of being in his arms.

"Good. One or two more." He gestured to her. "Come look at the images. See what you think and we can adjust."

She left the chaise and kicked out of her high-heeled shoes. She'd never been good at walking in such thin heels. Now barefoot, she joined him behind the camera.

"Well?" Luke moved aside and rested his hand on the small of her back. "I hope you approve."

She peered at the images in the LCD screen. He'd captured her in deep shadow and bright contrast, creating a sexy but elegant image. The portrait wasn't like anything created for the other members of the royal family.

"Well?" Luke rubbed her bare back. "Good?"

"They're beautiful." She traced the edge of the screen. "It's hard to believe these are of me."

"They are," he murmured. "They're how I see you. Beautiful, mysterious and almost out of reach."

She forgot about the camera. "I missed you. I wanted to run away, but I knew they'd find me." She slid her palm over his cheek. "I hated leaving you behind."

"I know." He enfolded her in his embrace.

"Charlie said to trust him." Emotion thickened her voice. "I've tried to come up with ways to get back to the States."

He petted her hair. "Your brother told me to trust him and he'd get me here. We're not out of the woods, but we have a few moments. Your folks don't know I'm on the grounds to be more than a photographer. When they find out, they'll be pissed."

He wasn't wrong, but that didn't mean she liked his line of reasoning. "We'll both be in trouble."

"It's a mess." He chuckled. "But look at us. You're in an evening gown and I'm in jeans. We shouldn't work."

"But we do." She wanted to go to her suite of rooms and be with the man she loved.

He kissed the tip of her nose, then along her jaw to her cheek and earlobe. "I should've married you when I had the chance."

"You want to?" She couldn't believe it. "Luke?"

"I do." He grinned. "I've never loved anyone in the way I love you."

She opened her mouth to reply, but the words evaporated. He'd shocked her. She loved him, too and needed to tell him.

Corinne hurried into the room. "We have a big problem." Her eyes widened. "Big. Huge."

"What?" Zara refused to leave Luke's side. "What's wrong?"

"Duke Elmore went to your parents and demanded your hand in marriage," Corinne said. "He made a formal request."

Oh shit. Zara trembled. She refused to marry the duke, but he was the only one her parents would approve.

Luke cleared his throat. "Miss Corinne?"

"Lady," Zara corrected. "She's still my lady."

"Lady Corinne? Please take the camera to Prince Charles' office." Luke grasped Zara's hand. "Please?"

"You take Princess Zara to her suite," Corinne said.

"Done." Luke nudged Zara, forcing her to move. She wanted to be free of Elmore, but this wasn't the way she'd envisioned running off with Luke. With Luke leading the way, she ran across the hall to her suite. She slammed the door shut. "Jesus."

"I'm sorry." He directed her to the bedroom. "You weren't kidding about Elmore. Has he always been this persistent?"

"Always." She settled on the bed. "For as long as I've known him. Will you unzip me? I can't breathe in this corset."

"Sure." He tugged the zipper down. "Stand and I'll help you out of your dress."

She glanced over her shoulder as she rose to her feet. "I'd think you're trying to get me naked, but I started this."

"I'm not passing up the chance to see every inch of you." He tugged the satin and silk down her body, exposing her. "Fuck."

"I know. I hate corsets, but it's the only way for me to get into this gown." She picked up her dress and placed it across the back of her makeup chair. "Did you tell Corinne to select a dark color?"

"Black is elegant and sexy." He shrugged. "But the navy does work well with your skin color and to your strengths."

"I never thought I was pretty." She straddled his lap. "You seem to think I am."

"Because you are." He slid his hands across her backside. "I'm your loyal subject."

"You're silly." She draped her arms around his neck. "Good thing I like your silly."

"I like you." He squeezed her ass. "Your leg looks better than the last time I saw it." He curled his fingers under her chin. "I knew you weren't going to die, but I was scared I'd lose you."

"Never. I'm indestructible, but I don't want to talk about being shot." She caressed the hairs at the base of his skull. "At least I wore silky underwear this time.

The first night we were together, I wanted to look sexy, but I was so plain."

"You've never been plain." He kissed her. "You make me hard when you smile at me." He stroked her back. "I'm thinking of all the sexy ways to photograph and draw you like this."

"In my bed works." She wriggled on his lap. Good thing the corset had a zipper front. She pulled the tab, exposing her breasts.

"Fuck. I like." He buried his face in her chest.

She threaded her fingers in his hair. The freedom of being with him, with the one she loved, relaxed her. She pressed her breasts to his mouth and Luke didn't disappoint. He sucked on her nipple.

Tingles shot through her body as he unzipped the corset the rest of the way. The garment tumbled to the floor. She ground on his lap, loving the feel of the bulge in his jeans. Passion flowed through her veins. Her world righted because of him.

"God, I missed you," he said against her breast. "Missed you in my arms. In my bed."

"I missed being there." She ruffled his hair, delighting in the softness of the strands.

He kept her in his arms and stood long enough to deposit her on the bed.

"Luke?" She reclined beneath him.

"Need you." He hooked his fingers in the elastic of her panties and dragged the flimsy silk down her legs. "Wet for me?"

"Yes." She craved him. She splayed her knees, opening to him. No fear or anxiety in baring her body, just love and acceptance.

His eyes glittered. He nuzzled her inner thigh, sending electric sparks across her skin. He scraped his teeth along the outer folds of her pussy, eliciting a moan from deep in her being.

"Touch me." She held on to her knees. "Luke."

He didn't speak. Instead, he slid one hand over her ribs to her chest. He buried his face in her pussy, caressing her folds with his tongue.

She let go of her knees and palmed his head. He knew how to bring her to the pinnacle. She ground on his face, urging him on. Heat coiled in her belly. Her legs trembled. The orgasm had built too quickly, but she couldn't fight the good feelings. She was putty in his hands.

He eased one finger into her cunt, probing her. When he curled his digit, she cried out. Nothing had ever felt this explosive or exciting in her life.

He hummed against her clit. "Tell me you love this."

She would if the words were there. No such luck. She opened her legs more and writhed. No thinking. Just feeling.

He pumped his finger in time with her bucking and alternated between soft touches and plucking her nipple.

Her restraint held by a thread. Now that she'd experienced the pleasure of orgasm, she wanted to do it again and again. The climax improved each time she felt it. She shivered. "Luke," she managed. Her body vibrated as the orgasm washed over her.

"Holding me in," he said. "So beautiful. Come for me and let go."

She wouldn't argue if she could. She shuddered around his finger and against his mouth. Her limbs loosened and the floaty feeling returned. She sagged on the bed.

Luke added a few more licks before he withdrew. He kissed her inner thigh.

Her skin tingled again. She felt beautiful and loved.

"Need you." He unbuttoned his shirt and whipped the garment off. He shoved his pants and boxers to the floor and stroked himself. "Love you, Zara."

He'd said the words. Although her brain was still fogged from sex, she knew what she'd heard. "Luke."

He crawled on the bed and settled between her thighs. "Next time, I'll teach you new positions. Right now, I can't wait." He pushed into her in one thrust.

Stars seemed to explode behind her eyelids. She belonged to Luke. He'd joined them as one heart, soul and body. She'd never be the same. The rest of the world and all her troubles didn't matter because she had this moment. She rocked into him, savoring every thrust. He knew how to touch her to her core. He'd seen her secrets and anxieties, but didn't push her away. He heightened her securities and freed her.

Luke grasped her hips. "Fuck. So tight and perfect." He gritted his teeth. Perspiration glittered on his chest. His nipples beaded and his movements turned feral.

She rolled him on top of her, kissing Luke.

He trembled. He broke the kiss and planted his forehead against hers. "Can't. Hold. Back."

"Come for me," she murmured. "Do it."

This time, he cried out and slammed into her. He shuddered, even as he added more thrusts.

Warmth flooded her body. She tucked her legs around him and whimpered. What a perfect moment.

He buried his face against her neck and stayed within her. "I love you, Zara. Forever."

She wanted to bottle this moment, so romantic and wonderful. "You're mine."

Time seemed to stop and she reclined with him. The silence enveloped them and she basked in the splendor of being with him. Having Luke as hers could be possible. She'd make him her partner and husband.

Luke withdrew and collapsed beside her on the bed. He kicked out of his bunched-up jeans and underwear. Once nude, he dragged a blanket over them. "I'm bound to call you my princess."

"Because you work here?" She found her strength and rolled onto her side. She hooked her leg across his and slipped her palm over his chest. "Or another reason?"

"I do work here, and it's the official way I should address you." He tangled up with her. "But that's not the full reason."

"No?"

"I gave up my degree to follow you," he said. "I did it because it was the only way."

"Luke." He couldn't do that. He deserved to finish. "You wanted that degree and to show your paintings in the galleries."

"I did." He petted her hair. "But my priorities changed."

"Oh?" She tensed. Did he now want her title?

"I was forbidden to see you and I'm probably going to be thrown out of the country, but your brother saw something in me. He's the one who helped me get here. Without him, I'd be rudderless in Kenton. My art would've suffered because my muse came to Lysianna."

"Charlie?" She didn't quite believe her ears. "Wait, your muse?"

"You." He trailed his fingers down her cheek. "When the family finds out Corinne and I are here, we'll most likely be tossed. She might get to stay because she's got your brother's royal command to do so. I'm not so lucky because I'm not a resident. Doesn't matter. My heart will always be right here." He drew a circle over her heart. "I love you, Zara. Not the princess side or the things you can do for me, but for the woman you are. You captivated me from the moment I saw you on that balcony."

"Luke." He said the right things and touched her heart. She loved him and couldn't see her existence without him.

"Coming here was a risk and I don't regret a second." He kissed her. "You're my princess."

Her voice disappeared. The words were there, but she couldn't speak to tell him the truth — she loved him.

"I didn't think you'd say anything right now. I understand." He sighed. "You think I'm like the rest. You think I want something from you and because I took this job, it's to get something out of this relationship. What I want is you. That's it. Nothing more."

Something thumped on the door. "Zara? It's Charlie."

Shit. Zara scrambled up from the bed and grabbed a robe. "Just a moment."

Luke rubbed his eyes. "I'm going to be escorted out." He left the bed and dragged his jeans up his legs. "Fuck. I knew this was too good to be true."

"No." She tied the belt on her robe. "It's not over. Just…" She'd figure something out. "Charlie?" She opened the door a crack. "Yes?"

"The jig is up," Charlie said and pushed into the room. He shut the door behind him. "They know."

"We have to buy time. I need to get him out of here so he's safe." She massaged her forehead. "This is my problem and it's time I stood up for myself."

"Too late." Luke paled. "Fuck."

Guards pushed into the room and knocked Charlie over. One pushed Zara out of the way. She tried to stop them as they grabbed Luke, but her size was no match for the sheer number of guards.

"Stop," she shouted. "I command you as your princess. Stop."

"Sorry, Princess. We have orders from the queen." The guard snapped handcuffs on Luke. "This man is charged with unlawfully entering the country and endangering the life of our princess."

"No." She grabbed the guard's arm, but he outmuscled her. "He saved me. Listen to me," she screamed. "He saved me from being killed when I was attacked. Please listen to me."

Luke, shirtless and barefoot, bowed his head. Without a word, the guards removed him from her suite.

One of the guards remained. "He's being charged with defiling the princess. I'm sorry."

Charlie found his footing and ran to Zara. He embraced her. "I'm sorry, kid. I tried."

"I know." She sobbed. She wasn't sure what else she could do. She wanted Luke back. He had not only her heart, but she knew he wasn't guilty. She loved him.

"Mother's coming," Charlie said. "I'm not leaving, but brace yourself. She's pissed and she'd got the duke on her side."

She assumed as much. "I'm ready." She had no other choice. If she wanted Luke, she had to put everything on the line. Luke mattered. Her future mattered. She'd found the first man outside of her brother to love her unconditionally. She loved Luke, too and refused to let him pay for something he hadn't done.

Chapter Twelve

Zara sighed and pieced together the first germ of a plan. If she was going to get Luke out of prison, then she'd have to put herself on the line. First, she needed to put on regular clothes. She might be a princess, but she didn't buy into the frippery and finery of the role. She'd rather be Zara, art student. "Give me five minutes to get properly dressed," Zara said. "I refuse to face my stepmother in a robe."

"She won't get in." Charlie hit the locks on the door. "And the camera is safe with me. I locked it up."

"Did you?" She yanked a pair of jeans and a tunic from her dresser. "Did you look at his work?" She ducked into the bathroom to change. She refused to be caught in less than a full outfit in front of her stepmother. She donned her bra and panties, then the tunic and jeans. She needed to be accepted for the woman she'd become, not the image her stepmother had of her.

"I did," Charlie said. "It's good work. It's the most honest and authentic portrait of you. On one hand, you're the princess and covered in jewels, but on the other, you're just a woman who wants to look pretty and isn't sure she does—like almost every other woman out there. You're approachable, but the image makes you look trapped and the starkness works."

She emerged from the bathroom, then pulled the pins from her hair. "Almost ready." She hated undoing the work Corinne had done with her tresses, but the style didn't work with the clothes. She pulled the mass of curls up with an elastic.

"I don't know how you do it." Charlie grinned. "You managed to look not like you've just had sex, but like you're ready to hit the books. You're better at the royal game than they think."

"That's the point."

Charlie crossed the suite. "Just know Mother and Father aren't listening to me, either. Mother won't let me access Father and he's not been seen all afternoon."

"Figures." She followed him to the door. "Father said I'd get bored when I went to college. I didn't get the chance to find out if I would or not. Mother shot down my idea of going and saying I needed Elmore to protect me. I did just fine. They don't trust me." She stepped into the corridor and spotted Oren. She nodded to her guard. "Any word on that shooting?" Her leg was nearly healed, but the fear wasn't gone.

"No, my princess." Oren dipped his head and tugged her aside. He gestured to Charlie.

Charlie joined the huddle. "What do you know?"

"We have the guy down in the pen. The duke's brother. He's a former Army Ranger. He was able to make the shot and is loyal to his brother. He thought he'd scare you into running to the duke," Oren said, his voice barely above a whisper. "Duke thought you'd go home and want to hide with him because you were scared. You weren't supposed to get hit."

"Not supposed to be *hit*?" Charlie asked. "She could've been *killed*."

"I won't run to him now." Zara folded her arms. "What are they doing with Luke?"

"He's in the jail, too." Oren nodded. "There are cameras down there—audio and visual, so you can keep an eye on him. As for the duke, he's denying he had anything to do with the shooting, but he's convinced you agreed to marry him. Your stepmother agreed for you."

Zara held up her hand. "Oh, hell no, I'm not marrying him. I get a say in this and I say no." She shook her head. "He offered me a bracelet, but it's not enough. Nothing would be enough."

"He wants to be the father of the future king," Charlie said, his voice thick. "So he can manipulate the child."

"Not my child." She sighed. "You said there are cameras on the jail? The brother is in custody?"

"He is," Oren said. "Luke is safe and in one of the nicer cells, but he is in the castle jail."

"Lovely. It's dirty down there and full of vermin." She groaned to hide her displeasure. She wanted to go to her lover, not talk with the queen. Still, she needed a plan. "They want me to marry Elmore, right?"

"Zara." This time Charlie groaned. "You can't."

"I have an idea." She grasped Charlie's shirtsleeve. "Elmore wants a virgin," she murmured. "I'm not."

"Luke?" Charlie asked.

"Duh." He'd set up the chance for her to have a tryst with Luke. How could Charlie not know?

"What do you want to do?" Charlie asked. "Mother won't let you get out of this."

"Let me handle Mother." She'd figure something out. "Can Luke work on my portrait?"

"Not in jail," Charlie said. "But I have the memory card and camera."

"The unveiling of my portrait has been moved up, right?" she asked.

"It has," Oren said.

"Good." She turned to her brother. "Have my portrait printed. That's what I want them to display." She smoothed her shirt and found her courage. "I'm going to see Mother."

"Good luck," Charlie said.

"Thanks." She strode down the corridor to meet her stepmother. She spotted the queen at the end of the corridor. "Mother?" She hurried to the far end of the wing.

The queen nodded and stepped into the sitting room. The space had been intended to be used as a playroom for the future grandchildren. Unless Luke got out of prison, there wouldn't be any.

Zara followed Eloise into the room.

"Close the door," the queen snarled.

Zara did as told. When the door snicked shut, she faced the matriarch. "Mother."

"You're back." Her stepmother settled on the couch and folded her hands on her lap.

"I am."

"You brought someone. Feeling charitable?"

"He's a fine artist. His work has been shown all over." Her words weren't a total lie—he must've had work shown somewhere.

"Where?"

Damn. "I'm not entirely sure. He's prolific."

"Right." Her stepmother sneered at her. "He will be removed."

She'd assumed so, but not if she could help it. "I'm an adult, Mother. I can make my own choices."

Her stepmother glared at her, but her position on the sofa remained stiff and proper. "You've made poor choices. You put yourself in danger and could've died. You went out in public without a guard. Do you know how that looked for the crown? For the people? It looked reckless. It made you appear careless and that you don't abide by the rules. Your people feel let down."

"They do? How?" she asked. "I'm finding my way so I can be the best monarch possible." Why didn't her stepmother and the people understand that? Probably not. She'd never met her birth mother and wondered if she'd have acted this way.

"You let them down because they want a glamourous princess. They want you to jet set and be the example," her stepmother snarled. "They don't want you to lower yourself to that...*artist.*"

She seethed, but she needed to buy herself time. What her stepmother claimed sure sounded like the family wanting to keep up appearances. Did the people care if she were glamourous or not? She doubted it, but her stepmother wouldn't be moved. "Fine. What do you expect me to do?"

"Use your head." Her stepmother folded, then refolded her hands. "We have an image to uphold. You will stop wearing...*that,* and act like a princess." She curled her lip in a sneer. "You look like a commoner."

She bit back a groan. "How do I act as you suggest?"

"Stop being so forthright. You're a demure princess," her stepmother said. "No one wants a blunt princess. They want quiet, correct beauty."

Not going to happen. She'd found freedom and liked having her own mind. "Okay." She folded her arms. "What else?"

"Stop being so independent. You're a royal. You need to follow the rules. My rules," her stepmother said. "Duke Elmore has asked for your hand. This Sunday, the official announcement will be made at your portrait unveiling. You have two days to correct yourself."

She winced. *Correct myself. Jesus.* She measured her breaths to keep her anger under control. "You've accepted his proposal."

"We did. He's the most suitable husband. He knows royal protocol and will fit in with the family," her stepmother said. "He wants what's best for the crown."

"The king agreed to this? Without my consent?" Her father could be cool and unapproachable, but this was a lot, even for him.

"He has agreed." Her stepmother toyed with a bracelet around her wrist. The jewels caught the light and Zara's attention. Rubies. "That's a pretty bracelet. What are the stones?"

"Rubies." Her stepmother smiled. "From a dear friend."

"Father?" She'd seen that bracelet before. "Elmore gave me a bracelet just like that one."

Her stepmother's eyes widened for a split second, then the thin smile returned to her face. "Mine came from a dear friend. Now, I have a meeting. I trust you've seen things my way. Yes?"

"Of course. I need to redirect my behavior and realize my role." She nodded. "I will."

"And at the announcement ball? You will act with decorum? This will be a big day for you and we cannot have an outburst." Her stepmother's sneer returned. "There won't be any unpleasantness, will there?"

"I'll behave." She needed to do a bit more digging, but she had her plan. "Thank you, Mother."

"I knew you'd see this my way." Her stepmother stood and resumed fingering the bracelet. "I've assigned you a new lady-in-waiting. You will select an appropriate gown for the announcement. The duke prefers red, so make sure it's red."

"I will, Mother." She followed the queen from the room. She couldn't spy on her stepmother on her own, but others could.

Once the queen was out of earshot, Zara leaned against the wall. "What are you hiding, Mother?" she murmured. "I'm not playing your game any longer. Luke's life depends on me and I won't let him down."

* * * *

Luke stared at the wall of his cell. *Fuck*. He'd landed in jail. Not entirely a surprise. He'd broken the rules. A commoner couldn't be with a princess and he'd aimed high. Sure, he hadn't known she was a princess when he'd fallen for her, but that didn't matter now. He loved Zara and didn't regret a second of their time together.

Then there was him allowing her brother to bring him to Lysianna. He probably should've thought his choice through a bit more. The chances he'd land in jail were high. Now, jail was his reality.

"Hey." The man in the cell across the corridor waved at him. His face was obscured in shadow, but his voice clear. "You're that guy."

"Yeah, I'm that guy." He had no idea what the man wanted or what guy he thought Luke might be.

"You're in here, too." The guy moved to the door of his cell, making his face more visible. "You're weren't supposed to make it this far."

"Well, I'm a champ." He couldn't contain his sarcasm. "You're in here, too."

"I should be. I shot at you." He laughed. "Ain't it a bitch? I shoot at you and we're both in the clink."

"You did what?" Luke paid closer attention. *Shot at me? What the hell?* "Where?"

"You should close your curtains, man. I saw right into your room." The man leaned on the cell door, resting his elbows on the bars. "She's cute. Did you get all of 'em naked before you porked 'em?"

Oh God. "She modeled for me." Did this jackass mean the princess was cute? "Why'd you shoot at me? I don't know you." He faked a laugh. "Did I steal your girl?"

"Not mine," the man said. "Elmore's girl. You took his piece of ass."

"The princess?"

The man laughed this time and the sound echoed. "Yeah. He can't stand her, but he'd be in line to be the king. The bastard. He's been doing the queen, too. At least she likes him."

"You're joking." *Shit.* Elmore was a real piece of work. "He doesn't like the princess?"

"She's difficult," the man said. "He'd rather have a more agreeable girl."

Luke gritted his teeth to keep from saying anything. The gall. Elmore didn't deserve Zara.

"I couldn't believe he wanted me to kill her, but he said she wasn't going along with the plan so she had to go. Even the queenie signed off on the plan," the guy said. "They knew."

"She did?" He couldn't wrap his mind around the sheer disgust concerning the situation. "You didn't kill the princess."

"No shit. I ain't goin' down for murder and I sure as hell won't go down for whacking a royal." He shrugged. "I hit her, didn't I? I'm sorry. I know it doesn't fix anything and won't get my ass outta here, but I apologize. This whole thing never should've gone that far. I'm not that cold, really. It was just he promised me good money and I needed it. You know? I've got kids and my ex wanted money."

"You hurt and scared the fuck out of her. Would you want someone to shoot at your kids? It's the same difference." Luke wanted to rip this man limb from limb, but he also wanted to keep him talking. Once he got out, he'd find Elmore and expose the bastard. "She bled pretty bad."

"Fuck. I never thought about it that way." The man stopped talking. "They're coming."

Guards filtered down the corridor and Luke pressed himself against the back of his cell. *Christ.* Were they there for him?

"The queen wishes to address the prisoners," one of the guards shouted. He opened the door to Luke's cell. "Bow."

Luke dropped to his knees. He'd never met a queen before. What was protocol? He glanced up and an older woman, clad in a crimson silk pantsuit, strode into his cell.

"Leave," she said. "The prisoner and I need to have a chat."

He didn't look up a second time and didn't speak. He refused to do much talking anyway so he didn't incriminate himself.

"You thought you were smart," she said. "Thought you found a meal ticket. My daughter isn't a means to your end." She threaded her fingers into Luke's hair and yanked, forcing her to look up at her. "Pity, really. You're handsome. She did choose someone with the features to be a royal, but you're not good enough. She should be with a man who can keep her in her proper place within society."

He disagreed, but she wouldn't listen to him even if he tried to speak.

"When the judge sees you, I expect you to admit your guilt and leave the country. Understand me? You will not destroy her public image. She's marrying the duke. You will not be part of her life, ever." The queen narrowed her eyes. "Or there will be consequences."

"Yes, Queen." The more she pulled, the more his scalp ached, but he refused to show his pain.

"Good boy." She let go. "If you weren't trying to climb the social ladder on my daughter's back, I'd take you as my lover." She crinkled her nose. "Pity, really."

He'd never sleep with her. The evil streak in her soul was more than he could take.

The queen knocked on the wall. "Leaving." She flicked her hand. "This one can stay through Sunday because I want him to experience the agony of the princess accepting the duke's proposal of marriage. Maybe then this one will understand he's not welcome here." She left without a backward glance.

Luke's stomach churned. He had too much information to digest and not enough time to get the situation sorted out. He needed to speak to Zara and Charlie. Did they know their stepmother was having an affair?

"You." The guard pointed to Luke. "Time for your shower."

He didn't feel like a shower. Luke remained on the floor of his cell. "I'm fine."

"You need this shower," the guard said. "You do."

Damn it. He hated being forced to comply. He stood, though, and trudged to the bars. "What if I'm fine?" He met the gaze of the guard. His voice lodged in his throat. Oren? "I'll shower." If Oren was there, then something was up. He allowed Oren to cuff him once the cell was opened again.

Oren escorted Luke down the other end of the jail to a room filled with harsh light. Charlie and Zara stood against one wall.

Luke wanted to embrace Zara, but not while being cuffed.

Zara rounded the table and hugged Luke. "I'm sorry."

He kissed the side of her head. "I know."

Charlie sat on the closest chair and tossed his phone onto the table. "You met our stepmother."

"I did," Luke said. "It was interesting."

Oren unlocked the cuffs. "Don't make me use these again so fast." He stood in front of the door, blocking anyone looking in through the window.

Luke nodded.

Zara kept her arms around Luke. "Ignore Mother. She's trying to scare you."

It had worked. Luke willed himself to stop freaking out. "She threatened me."

"We assumed so." Charlie rubbed his mouth with the back of his hand. "She's not going to touch you or throw you out."

"No," Zara added. "She won't."

"She's having an affair with Elmore," Luke blurted. "She admitted it." Getting those words out lightened some of the weight on his mind, but he hated having to be the one delivering the information.

Charlie's brows rose. "She admitted it?"

"Yes. She wanted me to be her lover, but turned me down because of Zara," Luke said. "Also because I wouldn't be with her."

"I had a feeling this was happening." Zara rubbed Luke's back. "She didn't admit it to me, but she gave herself away with the bracelet."

Luke stared at Zara. "You're oddly calm about this whole situation." He didn't understand.

"My stepmother has done backhanded and underhanded things since I can remember," Zara said. "Father can be dismissive, but Mother's just mean. She and my father couldn't have children, so she could even argue we're not the rightful ones—although I have no idea who might be instead."

"Anything is possible with her." Charlie fiddled with his phone. "Hot damn. She either forgot about or never knew about the security system down here." He held up his phone. "We have Mother's conversation with you."

"It records everything?" Luke asked. "Like chats between the prisoners?"

"Who talked?" Zara asked. "Luke?"

"The guy across the corridor. He says he's the one who shot Zara. He admitted it. Said the duke wanted to remove her—I don't know why Elmore wanted it, but he ordered the attack," Luke said. "The shooter refused to kill her." He'd been able to tell them the truth as he knew it and his spirits lifted. "That's what I know and it should be on your footage."

Zara continued to rub his back. "I knew it wasn't random."

He rested his forehead on her temple. "Are you accepting his proposal of marriage?"

"Elmore's? No." She turned her head and brushed her nose against his. "There's this artist I like and I can't marry the wrong man."

Her words were breadcrumbs, but good enough for him. He needed the lifeline.

Charlie tapped his phone. "Found it. Crisp audio, too." He grinned. "Saved and secure."

"Can I go?" Luke asked. He wanted to return to her suite for a proper shower and to make love to Zara.

"Not yet," Zara said. "We have the confession and my stepmother dead to rights, but I have to out Elmore. Until then you need to stay here, but Oren will be on guard for you."

"I need to handle this," Charlie said. "No sex, you two." He grinned, then ducked through a door at the back of the room.

Zara nuzzled Luke's cheek. "I don't like leaving you here. It's killing me."

"It's not a thrilling time, no." He embraced her properly and breathed in the scent of her perfume. He missed holding her. "I'll survive because it means I'm getting back to you."

"You still want me?" She leaned back in his arms and her eyes shimmered.

"I do." She made his life worthwhile and interesting. "I can't finish my series without you."

"I guess not." She caressed his back. "Give me the chance to free you and I will. I'm not letting the duke win. Ever."

"I know." He breathed her in and she calmed him. He admired her strength and bravery. "You got yourself to college, to a new country, and will outsmart Elmore. I know it."

Oren cleared his throat. "Time to return to your cell."

"Oren's going to be your guard, so no one will hassle or hurt you," she said. "When I call for you, trust me, okay?"

"Anything for you." He'd give everything to have her in his arms again.

"Won't be long now." She let go. "Luke."

"I love you." He allowed Oren to recuff him and take him to his cell. He didn't feel like an inmate any longer. He had a role to play and he'd do it because Zara was his reward. She'd be in his arms and his life would be right.

Soon.

Chapter Thirteen

Zara adjusted the bodice of her dress and fiddled with the sequins along the neckline. If she was going to be the center of attention, then she wanted to wear something she liked. Elise, her new lady-in-waiting, placed the thin crown on Zara's head. Zara liked her. Elise seemed sweet and eager, but rather young. If she had her preference, Zara would rather have Corinne, but she wasn't in a position to argue. Besides, she had to get ready for the announcement ball.

Sunday had come too fast, but she hadn't come up with another way to prevent the dreaded upcoming proposal from Elmore.

She checked her makeup in her reflection in the mirror. She did look nice. "Corinne made me look better than ever. Don't you think?"

"She did, my princess," Elise said. "You'll be the prettiest woman there."

"Don't let the queen hear you say that." Zara left the chair. "She'll have your head." She wanted to sound joking, but the queen wasn't a fan of being upstaged.

Elise paled. "She will."

"Stop. I won't let her remove you." She smoothed her dress again. She'd chosen a black cocktail dress with a flair skirt and square neckline. The gown reminded her of a flirty fifties party dress. She paired the garment with kitten heels. The crown seemed almost out of place against the rest of her outfit.

Elise clicked the diamond bracelet on Zara's wrist. "Will you be wearing a ring?"

"Yes." She selected a thick band embedded with diamonds, given to her on her eighteenth birthday, for her left hand and a sapphire ring for her right hand. Just enough to be sparkly without going overboard.

"Beautiful." Elise's smile wavered. "Next time, may I come with you to the ball?"

"Yes." If she weren't going to possibly blow up her life in the next few hours, she'd have Elise join her. "The next time you'll be right beside me."

Elise brightened. "You should go. Duke Elmore will be here soon and if you wish to avoid him, then you'd better leave now." She nodded. "I hope you don't marry him. He's…icky."

"Icky?" Interesting way to put it.

"I shouldn't talk."

"Go ahead. You're in safe company." She tipped her head. Going to college and getting out of the kingdom had opened her eyes. She'd learned listening skills and how to better handle the problems of her people before making a choice. "Elise?"

"He told me he's part of the court and he'd take me to bed." Elise trembled. "He's old enough to be my father. You won't remove me, will you? I shouldn't have spoken up."

"You've helped me make my decision because I appreciate knowing the truth. You will be my lady for quite a while." She hugged her lady. "Thank you for being honest."

"Thank you?" Elise's eyes widened. "My princess?"

"Why don't you head down to the kitchen and sneak into the party? I won't tell and I'd be happy to know you're there." She winked at her lady. "I'm ready."

"Thank you." Elise bowed. "Have a good evening."

Zara left the suite and headed down to the foyer of the grand ballroom. Charlie and Corinne were already there. Charlie left Corinne by the doors. "Are you ready?" he asked. He hugged her. "You're going to be great."

"I hope so." She sighed and composed herself. "Is everyone in place?" She'd never been good at following the rules of presentation. She liked to go into the room, not be announced and have all eyes on her. Tonight, she had to be on her best behavior.

"The package is and the portrait is ready." Charlie squared his shoulders. "Nothing stopping us now."

"Okay." She flexed her hands. *We can do this.* "Thanks for bringing Corinne along. I know it's killing you not to have your boyfriend."

"Don't have a boyfriend right now and tonight is about you. She's your friend and she makes me laugh. I'm not going to marry her, but at least we've got someone on our side. You know?" Charlie grinned. "This is your shot, and I won't get in the way."

Corinne waved to Charlie. "Your turn."

As his name was called, Charlie descended the stairs with Corinne on his arm. Zara measured her breaths to compose herself again. She couldn't look scared, but she wished she'd been able to make her entrance with her brother. She kept an eye out for Elmore. The last thing she needed was for him to show up.

She focused on her mission — getting Luke out of jail and on with his life. Calling him the package irritated her, but whatever. This was about more than her.

The announcer gestured to Zara. Her turn. She moved to the top of the stairs. "Presenting, our princess, Catherine Zara Westbrook of Lysianna," the announcer said.

The light shined bright on her. The sequins of her dress glittered. She eased down the steps and hoped she didn't trip or fall. Once on solid ground, she curtsied to her stepmother, father and brother. She took her place next to Corinne and allowed herself to breathe. The lights seemed brighter than she remembered and the music louder. She didn't know a damn thing about classical pieces, but the one the quintet played bounced along at a good clip. Gold bunting had been affixed to the ceiling in long swoops. Gold flowers festooned each table and jeweled vases overflowed with white roses and vibrant pink lilies. The crown on Charlie's head glittered. Even Corinne wore sparkly clips in her hair. Her father's crown sat regal on his head, but the circles under his eyes seemed deeper. The conversation remained low and people mingled around her. Part of her wanted to run, but the rest of her insisted she see this through.

Other people arrived at the ball, but Zara paid them little mind. She wanted to get through the evening as soon as possible. She shook hands and curtsied to visiting dignitaries. When Duke Elmore approached, she bristled. His tuxedo fitted nicely and to anyone watching from the sidelines, he seemed dashing, too. His nice exterior hid his rotten core.

"Elmore." She refused to offer her hand. The less he touched her, the better.

"Dance with me." He grasped her fingers anyway. "We need to make this look good."

Sure we do. "Of course." She allowed him to drag her out to the middle of the floor. A string quintet played a softer song, one better for dancing to. She kept space between her and Elmore as they danced. She'd rather get rid of him, but first, they had to have a conversation. "You're here."

"I am and you look lovely, but you'd have stood out better in red. The black is so morbid." He patted her ass. "Next time, you'll do as I request."

She moved his hand. "I'll keep that in mind." She allowed him to whisk her around the floor. "You expect me to accept your proposal."

"Your stepmother already agreed for you." He resumed touching her ass. "Doesn't matter what you say now. Deal's done."

"I see." The tingles she felt with Luke weren't there when Elmore touched her ass. Nothing from this man reminded her of her artist. She dug her nails into Elmore's hand. Time to corner him. "Before or after you slept with my stepmother?"

"Princess." He didn't miss a step, but his eyes flashed. She'd touched a nerve. He yanked her close. The muscle in his cheek twitched, yet he regained his poise. "That's not for discussion here, but I'm not with your stepmother that way."

"You're special friends," she said.

"Yes. We're close confidantes."

"Who exchange gifts?"

"Princess. You need to remember your position," he snapped. "You're not here to make choices. Your parents want the best for you."

"I know." She stopped dancing. "Never give me the exact same bracelet you gave my stepmother." She turned on her heel and walked away. When she reached the royal table, Elmore caught up to her.

"I knew college would turn you," Elmore said. "You were agreeable before."

She lowered her voice and measured her words. "You are sleeping with my stepmother. She told me as much, which means she's cheating on my father and he deserves better."

"Stop." His lip curled in a sneer. "You're out of line."

"I am? Who are you to decide that for me? If she's sleeping with you, then I will not marry you. No." She kept her voice level. "Leave me alone."

"You'll change your mind." Elmore snorted. "We'll make a baby and you won't have to deal with me, but mark my word, we *will* get married."

"No, we won't." She left the table in search of her brother.

Charlie was dancing with Corinne in the middle of the throng of people. Both seemed happy. Zara's heart pricked. She wanted that kind of joy, but wished they had their own respective happiness.

"Catherine." Her stepmother grabbed her arm. "A word?"

"Mother." She stopped at the edge of the room. For a split second, when she looked into the crowd, she thought she saw Luke. Could he be there? He'd been freed?

The queen directed Zara to a quiet corner away from the media and attendees. "You've turned down the duke."

"It's not breaking news." She swept her gaze over her stepmother. The queen tended to wear cream or champagne colored gowns. Tonight, she wore a crimson sheath dress, encrusted with rhinestones. She sparkled with each movement and the gown ensured she'd grab attention. Zara would be willing to bet the gown cost a fortune.

"He's the only dignitary willing to marry you. You've managed to alienate the rest of them." The queen narrowed her eyes. "Don't you know you're difficult? Men want a woman who can do what they want."

"He's sleeping with you," Zara snapped.

"Rumors and lies," her stepmother said, dismissing her.

She wanted to play that game? *Fine.* Zara would play. "He tried to have me killed and *you* knew about it."

"Impossible." Her stepmother's gaze remained granite still.

"Why would the shooter, who is in custody, but might not be now, tell anyone within listening range that he'd done it and you signed off on the job?" Zara asked. "That's not something anyone would say off the cuff."

"Lies."

"Started by?"

"Everyone wanting to bring down the family."

"It was you." She sighed. "Ever since you married my father, you've acted like the world is out to get you and you have to be angry first. I don't care what you want any longer. This isn't about you. It's not about me being a good wife or proper royal who follows the line and doesn't argue. It's about the family and the country." She spotted her brother by the royal portraits. "I have to leave. It's time for the big reveal." She paused as realization hit. "You want to save face, don't you? You're pushing hard to make everything look good, but it's rotten and I'm done. We're royals and we need to start acting like it. Why? It's time to show off my portrait." She sidestepped the queen and headed to the portrait gallery.

"Catherine." The king stopped her. "Are you enjoying yourself?" He escorted her to the line of photographs and paintings.

"No." She stood next to her father. "I'm not."

"What isn't up to your liking?" the king asked. "Tell me and it will be amended."

She summoned her courage. "I know who tried to kill me." Everything around her seemed to go quiet, but the blood thumped in her ears. She balled her hands to keep from showing the trembling.

He nodded once. "Come with me." He stepped behind the velvet rope and walked to the back of the royal dais, away from listening ears and prying eyes. "Talk to me."

She had his full attention? She hadn't been granted that in a long time and she refused to squander the chance. "First, the queen is cheating on you with Duke Elmore. I know because he gave us the same gift and when questioned, she admitted it," Zara said. "It's messed up."

The king folded his arms. "There is no law forbidding her from taking a lover, but I'd hoped she'd reconsider. Next?"

He knew? And he'd been okay with the queen's antics? She forged ahead. "Second, I refuse to marry Elmore. If he's with her, then he's not going to bed me."

"Understood."

She'd made headway. "Third, Duke Elmore tried to have me killed. Charlie has the proof, but suffice it to say, the duke hired his brother to assassinate me in Kenton."

The king said nothing, but the muscle in his jaw flexed.

"Father, I cannot marry someone who wants me dead."

"No."

A lump formed in her throat. "They want to embarrass the crown tonight. To embarrass me. It's cruel."

"It is." The king held up his hand. "All will be well."

"Daddy?" She hadn't called him that in years. "I'm scared."

"You have nothing to fear." He smiled and dipped his head once. "I didn't do enough to protect you up to now, but you're proving to be quite skilled at reading people and sorting out motives. What do you want, Zara?"

"Want?" She sucked in a ragged breath. "I want Luke removed from the prison and freed. I want the man who did try to hurt me put in his place. I'd like to be able to move around the grounds without having to look over my shoulder, and to be happy. If I had my way, I'd like to return to college, too." It was too much to ask, but he wanted to know.

Before her father could answer, the queen stepped up to the royal portrait gallery and demanded attention.

"Ladies, gentlemen, family and friends. On this day, we mark the transition for Princess Catherine from princess to duchess. First, the royal portrait. Behind these curtains is the official portrait to both sum up and enhance the image of our dear princess," the queen said. "We are honored to add her likeness to the gallery."

Zara tensed. The queen spoke about her like she wasn't even there. She should be next to the portrait, but she didn't trust the queen not to do something terrible.

The queen pulled the rope, revealing the image. Zara smiled from the portrait. The stark black-and-white picture was a strong change from the other former images. She appeared nude and risqué, compared to the full-length fully clothed portraits before hers. But the image also screamed elegance and style.

"My God." The queen stood in front of the portrait. "This will be changed at once. She's naked." She opened her arms, trying to block the image. "I want this gone now."

"Queen, the portrait stays," the king bellowed. "Our daughter looks wonderful and modern. I like the unique quality of the image. It suits her."

The queen paled. "My King. It's unacceptable. She looks…like she's of ill repute."

"It stands. No question." The king folded his arms. "I'm told there is to be a proposal tonight. Is this still the case?"

Zara's stomach churned. If her father condoned this proposal like he had the portrait, she'd pass out.

Duke Elmore stepped forward. "My King. I ask most humbly and most lovingly for your daughter's hand in marriage. I wish to make her my bride and the happiest woman in the world. It will please me when she accepts."

The king stood tall. "Princess? What say you?"

She got a choice? "No."

"No?" The duke's smile tensed. "My princess. We're fated."

She glanced at the king, then focused on Elmore. She wanted to grill the duke, but her father had the most standing.

"Duke Elmore, you have asked for her hand, but I must ask if your heart is pure," the king asked. "Is it?"

"Pure and in love with the princess," Elmore said, his voice smooth. If he'd been unnerved, Zara couldn't tell now.

"Yet, it's come to my attention that you love another as well," the king said. "Which is the truth?"

"He loves Catherine," the queen said. She made her way to the dais. "Enough games. We agreed Catherine would marry the duke and should get the plans under way. This union should be blessed. It's fated."

"You made the choice without her consent." The king turned to Zara. "Correct?"

"Yes." Zara's heart hammered. Her father seemed to have heard her pleas.

The king addressed the crowd and Duke Elmore. "Until a very short time ago, I allowed the wrong people to advise me. I believed these people had the best interests of the crown at heart."

"My King." The queen joined him on the platform. "Stop this." She nudged Zara out of the way. "This union is best for the kingdom."

"No, it's not," Zara said. "He tried to kill me." Adrenaline thundered through her veins. The excitement of having the truth come out battled with her sadness. Being honest ruined so many lives.

Her stepmother gasped and Elmore glared.

"Duke Elmore, you have been accused," the king said. "I have evidence you indeed ordered the execution of my daughter. I have evidence, My Queen, that you knew about the plot. Now I've learned of your affair. Do you expect me to trust either of you with my life and that of my daughter? Guards, remove them from my sight."

Zara wobbled. *Shit.* Her father wasn't playing around.

The queen shrieked. "You would abolish me?"

"In a heartbeat," the king snarled. "You were chosen because you claimed to love me, but you took advantage of a grieving man with two small children. You claimed to love me and Lysianna, but you only love yourself. You wanted to be queen, not the mother of my children. Be gone from my sight. Guards, put the duke in the dungeon."

"My King." The duke paled. "I knew she wasn't a virgin. Your princess is tainted. She's not worthy to be queen, either. Ask her about the painter." He struggled against the guards. "Ask her."

Zara balled her hands. Of course he'd make this about something other than his own transgressions. She accepted her shortcomings, but first, Elmore had to pay for his.

The queen wept as the duke was hauled from the room. "My King. Please reconsider. I made a mistake and deserve a second chance."

"I gave you a second chance when you bedded Sir Longstreth. I forgave you for your affair with Nial Roberts. I even looked the other way when you said you needed space, but were instead visiting Duke Katz. A queen should be loyal." The king pointed to the door. "Go."

Holy shit. Zara pressed her lips together. No wonder her father had lost his temper and thrown the queen out. She couldn't imagine cheating on Luke in such a manner.

The queen didn't speak as the guards led her from the ballroom.

The king sank onto his throne. "I want her royal portrait removed."

Zara nodded and accepted her fate. "Yes, Father. I'll have another taken."

"Not yours," he said. "The queen's." He flicked his fingers. "Music. Dancing. Now."

People filtered onto the dancefloor and the music resumed. The king grasped Zara's hand. "My daughter."

"Father." She sat beside him. "I'm sorry this all fell apart."

The king nodded once. "The young man who photographed you, the one you met in Kenton. He saved your life?"

"He saved me from blending into the background of life and tended to me when I was shot, yes." Hope blossomed in her heart. Maybe, just maybe, she could get Luke freed tonight. "He was being kept in the jail."

"He is the reason you're no longer a virginal princess."

She winced. "Yes." She bowed her head, averting her gaze. "I love him, Father."

"Does he love you?" the king asked.

"He does. Will you release him? I beg of you to please let him go," she said. "He did come here under false pretenses, but he did it for me."

"Prince Charles," the king bellowed and directed Charlie to the dais. Music continued to play and the people still danced. The king held up his hand. "Bring in the prisoner."

Prisoner? Zara scooted to the edge of her seat and focused on the main doorway. *Luke?*

Charlie stepped onto the platform. "He's no longer in jail, My King."

Zara stared at her brother. He had to be joking. "He's gone?"

"He's been released," Charlie said. "And he chose his own path."

Where would he go? She had to find him. Zara stood. "I…"

The king stood and silenced Zara. "I'm told there is another proposal to be made. Is this true?"

Another? Who now? Zara willed herself not to cry. If someone else asked her to marry them and wasn't Luke, she'd leave.

"My Lord." Luke strode through the crowd. "I have a proposal." He wore a simple black tuxedo and his smile stretched from ear to ear.

She blinked. Luke was there. He stood at the base of the royal platform. He'd come to her.

Luke dropped to one knee. "King, Prince, Princess? I offer my heart and soul to the princess and ask for her hand in marriage."

Zara left the dais and joined Luke on the main floor. "You're here."

"I am." He held a box. "When you were whisked away, a part of me went with you. I told you I love you because I do. I'm not a duke or a prince. I'm a humble artist who may never make enough money to keep you in the lap of luxury, but everything I have is yours. Heart, soul, body. I came here with the hope we'd be together." He opened the box. A ring with a dark blue sapphire lay nestled in the black velvet. "Will you marry me?"

Zara wanted to reach for him. Wanted to throw herself in his arms and never let go. Instead of answering him, the words escaped her.

"Princess?" The king strode off the platform. "This is what you wanted, is it not?"

Corinne nodded. "Zara?"

Luke smiled. "It's a lot to take in."

The king elbowed her. "You'd better accept this poor man's proposal, Zara. I've already blessed the union. He wouldn't be here if I hadn't."

This time, Charlie nodded. "He did. I know because I witnessed it."

"I thought he was going to execute me," Luke said. "Zara?"

She had everything she wanted. All she had to do was say yes.

"You deserve the marriage I thought I had for a second time," the king said. "One born of love and respect."

Zara enfolded Luke in her embrace. Holding him righted her world. "I'll marry you, yes."

"Yes?" Luke kissed her. "My princess?"

"Your Zara." Tears blurred at the corners of her eyes. "I will marry you and follow you to the ends of the earth." She'd run away to find her heart and found it in Luke's hands.

"Then we should celebrate," the king said. "A toast to my daughter, the princess, and her soon-to-be husband. Hooray!"

The room erupted in cheers as Luke removed the thick diamond band and slipped the engagement ring onto her finger. "I'll put this in my pocket," he said and tucked the other ring into his breast pocket. He kissed her again. "You had me worried."

"I did?" She clung to him as he walked her to the table. "I love you, Luke Cobb, so much."

"I love you, too." He stopped behind the table and away from the crowd. "It's true. They helped me set this all up. Charlie pled my case with the video and your father grilled me so much I wasn't sure I made him happy. I thought for sure they'd put me on the rack."

"He's tough to read sometimes." She gazed into his eyes. "I stood up to them. I found my backbone because of you."

"It was always there." He smoothed a loose lock of her hair behind her ear. "Dance with me?"

"Yes." She allowed him to walk her back out to the dance floor, then tucked into his embrace. "I can't wait to finish tonight so we can enjoy the rest of our evening—in bed." She'd been so lucky when she'd stepped onto the Kenton campus. She couldn't wait to start her life with him and show him how much she loved him.

"Where else?" Luke kissed her as they slow danced. "First, we should enjoy the party. You need the good time, and the kingdom needs some normalcy."

"You're right." Once the song finished, she made her way back to the dais and sat beside her brother.

The king stood. "Announcing the official engagement of Princess Catherine Zara to Luke Cobb, our royal photographer and artist. Raise your glass in a toast. Hooray!"

The crowd broke out in cheers.

She held tight to Luke's hand. The evening had started out awful and ended in the perfect way—well, mostly perfect.

"What's wrong?" Luke asked. "Don't you like me in a tuxedo? I'm lucky this one of Charlie's fit."

"He has five." She rested her head on his shoulder. "You look handsome and I'm the luckiest woman in the room."

"But?"

"I'm torn." She wasn't sure how to feel. Luke was by her side, but her mother and now stepmother weren't. Her mother had died, but her stepmother could've been the hero Zara needed. "How could the queen do that? How could she try to marry me to that rotten man?"

"I don't know," Luke said.

The king leaned back in his seat. "You've been told the queen and I weren't married out of love, yes?"

She paid rapt attention to her father. "Yes." She squeezed Luke's fingers. Her father didn't speak much about his personal life and if he wanted to talk, she'd listen.

"We weren't. She wanted a place in society and I thought I loved her. You and your brother mirror her in a lot of ways, even if she's not your biological mother. You've both got her cunning and craftiness. Unlike her, I trust you both. Charlie will be a fitting king and you, Zara, have the makings of a great advisor. You see what's the best for the people."

She sagged against Luke, honored by her father's words.

"Your stepmother cared only about herself. She tried to ingratiate herself to Charlie to ensure she'd never have to leave the court. She saw you, Zara, as nothing but the spare and a nuisance. Once the coronation happened, she froze me out. There was no love to begin with, but I kept hoping she'd change." The king shook his head. "She didn't."

"Daddy, I'm sorry." Knowing the truth and hearing it from him broke her heart.

"She picked the duke because she wanted to keep the traitor close for her own use. It never had anything to do with your happiness or him being the only suitable candidate," the king said. "You should marry the person who makes you happy and brings out the best in you. This country needs a court worthy of its citizens."

"You're worthy," she said.

"So is Charlie." The king sighed, but smiled. The weight seemed to leave his shoulders. "It'll be formal at the end of the month, but I'm stepping down and Charlie is going to be crowned. You and Luke will assist him."

"What about you?" she asked.

"It's time I found my heart's desire. I had it once with your mother and I've got the best children. You can handle the kingdom. But I need to be happy." The king nodded once. "It's time to step down."

"What about Corinne?" she asked. "It was a true mistake. Is she still banished?"

"No. She and Elisa are your ladies, but Corinne has the freedom to move in and out of the castle." The king left the table. "I must discuss my situation with my lawyer, but the queen is no longer part of the court."

Zara couldn't believe her ears. She'd gained everything she'd ever wanted and the bad actors were getting their just deserts.

Luke kissed her hand. "Would you care to dance again? We can't leave yet."

"Yes, please." She allowed him to lead her to the center of the room again. "You have no idea how happy I am."

"I bet I do." He held her close and his breath warmed her skin. "We fell into this pretty fast."

"We did." She rested her head on his shoulder. "My heart knew before my head made sense of this."

"Doesn't matter. We're here now and together." He nuzzled her hair. "Your father and brother grilled me for four hours, wanting to know my motivations for loving you."

"They wanted to be sure you love me." Being in his arms felt good. "Charlie should've trusted you."

"He did, but he got a cheap thrill out of seeing me squirm." He chuckled against her neck. "I didn't care what they did or said because I knew I'd be with you. That was enough reward." He held her tighter. "I've been truly hired as the court artist."

She leaned back in his embrace. "You have?"

"I was. Charlie paid me to finish the series I started," Luke said. "I'm not showing it in public, but it's done."

"You should make it public." It seemed a shame to keep his work under lock and key. "What will you do next?"

"I'm teaching art here in the kingdom to whomever wants to learn and you're going to head up the art museum. I'm told it's in sorry shape and needs someone who understands history to sort it all out. Charlie wants you to organize it."

Working at a museum did fulfill one of her dreams. "What about our degrees? We worked hard."

"We can finish those once Charlie finds his perfect man and can focus on the kingdom. He'll need your help to keep the country running smoothly," Luke said. "Your father is tired and wants a rest."

"We'll be a team." She held on to her man. "I got what I wanted — you. Now it's time my father and brother got the same."

"I'm all yours."

Chapter Fourteen

Luke couldn't keep his eyes open. He'd never danced and laughed so much in his life. The ball had been more than he expected, too. The noise, the lights, the sheer luxury of the event... Some of the gowns had to cost more than a car and the extravagance shocked him. But this was a kingdom and the crown possessed great wealth.

He yawned. He'd started the morning in jail. Now he wore a tuxedo and was engaged to the love of his life.

Zara patted his thigh. "Time to cash in. I want to go upstairs." She nodded to her brother. "Goodnight, Charlie, Corinne."

"Night," her brother said. "Behave."

She laughed, but Luke hesitated. "Thank you," he said. "Really."

Charlie half-shrugged. "Find me my happy ending and we'll be even." He waved. "Night."

Zara led the way back to her suite. She wore the tuxedo jacket, having stolen it when she'd gotten cold earlier in the evening, and the garment swallowed her frame. He couldn't wait to strip her down and kiss every inch of her body.

Once in her suite, Luke sighed. Being there was like coming home. He didn't believe he belonged in a castle. He wasn't born to have such luxury, but he knew his destiny and Zara was it. She closed the door and tossed her shoes onto the floor.

"Finally." She shrugged out of his jacket and eased into his arms. "You said you'd teach me new positions. We're alone and no one will interrupt us."

Electricity shot through his veins. "I did." He kissed her. "Follow my lead." He wanted to be inside her and make her fly.

"What are you going to do?" She nibbled on his chin. "Show me."

He would. He let go of her and tugged her to the bed. "Stand." He sat on the edge of the mattress with Zara between his knees.

"Now what?" When she reached for him, he stilled her hands.

"Trust me." Luke tugged the zipper of her dress. The garment parted and exposed her to his view. She wore a lacy strapless bra and matching black panties. The dress landed at her feet. His mouth watered. He could draw her right now. *Christ. So sexy and all mine.* He planted his mouth on her belly.

She whimpered and threaded her fingers into his hair. He swirled his tongue around her navel. He wanted to taste her everywhere. When she whimpered again, he slid one hand between her legs and caressed her pussy through the fabric of her panties. *Wet already.*

"Been thinking about me all day?" he asked against her stomach.

"All day." She caressed his head. "Luke."

He palmed her ass, loving the feel of her soft skin under his hand. She parted her legs, welcoming him.

"How do you know how to make me feel so good?" She shuddered. "I need you."

That was what he wanted to hear. Luke moved up her back to her bra catch and unhooked it. The lacy bra landed on the carpet with her dress.

Her nipples beaded, taut and rosy. Her skin glittered and she embodied every naughty fantasy he'd ever had just by standing before him. He latched onto her breast. The jolt of electricity shot through him. She tasted like wine and he was hooked on her.

"Luke." She arched into him. "Feels good." She ruffled his hair. "I need more."

He switched to her other nipple, hooked his fingers into the thin elastic of her panties and dragged the lingerie down her legs.

Zara tensed again. "Luke."

He parted her pussy lips and caressed her clit. When she jerked forward, he speared his digit into her cunt.

"Oh God." She grasped his shoulders. "Luke." She trembled and squeezed him from within. "More."

He switched nipples again. She tasted divine and he could nibble on her forever because she intoxicated him. Her cream coated his fingers. God, she was wet for him. He wanted to lick her pussy, but he might not last long enough to taste, then fuck her.

She writhed on his finger. "Fuck me." Another tremble rocked through her.

"Such a dirty mouth." He withdrew and grasped her hips. "On your knees." He needed her to prep him — not that it'd take long.

Desire filled her eyes. She sank to the floor and stared up at him and, without a word, opened his trousers. He unhooked his cummerbund and yanked his shirt free from his pants. His cock pressed against the fabric of his trousers.

She freed his dick from his underwear. Pre-cum shimmered on the blunt head of his erection.

"Want me?" he asked.

"Yes." She licked her lips. "Please?"

"Get me ready." He toyed with her hair, twisting a curl around his finger. When he stared into her eyes, he saw forever.

"Yes." She wrapped her fingers around his shaft, stroking and licking.

God, she was beautiful on her knees. She knew how to touch him in all the right ways. He loved her. "Yes." He guided her head. "Take me in." She overwhelmed him. His synapses misfired and he couldn't think straight. He needed her surrounding him, in and out of her heat.

Her hair tickled his legs. When she plunged down on him, he pushed deep. She took him to the back of her throat and swallowed.

"Holy fuck." Her move turned his senses inside out. His balls ached and he craved her. "Zara."

She fondled his sac. "Yes?" she asked between licks. "More?"

"God, yes." He jerked his hips. Everything centered on her.

She stopped licking him and her voice turned curt. "Don't you come until you're inside me. I want you in me."

His thoughts scattered at her commanding tone. Damn, she sounded so official and fucking sexy. "Yes." He wasn't sure he could hold back. He gritted his teeth. "Zara."

She withdrew again and sat back on her heels. "Good?"

"I'm gonna blow." He panted. "On the bed on your hands and knees. Show me your ass."

"Luke?" The flicker of concern shimmered in her eyes.

"I've got you." He let go of her hair. "You'll love it."

Zara scampered onto the bed. As she settled in place, she waved her ass.

"Naughty." He swatted her bottom. "You need me?"

"I do." She flipped her hair over her shoulder. "Fuck me."

"That's my girl." He stood behind her and rubbed his erection between her pussy lips, smearing her cream. He liked the forthright demand.

She whimpered. "Luke." A shiver rocked through her. "More."

"Not yet." Warmth surged through his body. Blood rushed to his cock and the need overwhelmed her. He lined himself up with her pussy and pushed. Inch by inch, he sank into her tight hole.

She squeezed him. When she glanced over her shoulder, the corner of her mouth kinked.

God, she was the sexiest woman alive. He grasped her hips. Nothing could stop him now. His heart belonged to her and she belonged to him. He lost himself in the simple pleasure of fucking her.

"Luke." She rocked back into him, meeting him thrust for thrust. He slid his palms along her ribs to her chest and tweaked her nipples.

Zara cried out. "Oh…" She trembled. "More."

He moved faster as the orgasm blossomed within him. He needed her to come with him. Luke abandoned her chest in favor of her clit. With each thrust, he rubbed her tender bud. The different angle sent him deeper into her body.

"More." She wriggled on her hips. "Luke."

He pushed to the hilt and pulled nearly out. He held tight to her hip and leaned over her as he massaged her clit.

"Luke." She shuddered. "Fuck." She flexed her cunt around him as she came.

Feeling and seeing her lose control destroyed his restraint. He surged into her with feral strokes. The more he leaned over her, the more they were one body moving in perfect rhythm. "Love you, Zara." He pushed hard as he hit his climax.

She buried her face in the bedding and moaned.

His sentiments exactly. No words were needed. He kissed her shoulder and knew he'd never be the same. She wore him out in every way and he loved it. His life revolved around hers. He threaded his arms about her waist and stayed in her pussy. This moment mattered more than anything because it made them one.

She sighed. "I felt you in my soul. Still do."

He couldn't answer in coherent sentences, not right now. "Uh-huh."

She laced her fingers with his and nuzzled the sheets. "This night went how I hoped but never dreamed was possible." She kissed his hand. "I love you, Luke."

"Love you, too, babe." He gathered his wits and pulled out. She'd worn him to a frazzle. He collapsed beside her on the bed.

She tangled up with him. "You were right. It felt very good."

"Yeah." He nipped her earlobe. "I've never lied to you." *Never will, either.*

"You haven't." She slid her arm across his belly. "You truly love me?"

"I do." His words came from his heart. "You mean everything to me. Princess or not, college girl or not, you're the one I want. I would be drawn to you. My soul knew you were my perfect match."

"You're mine, too." She kissed him. "You wore me out."

"Sleep, princess. I'll be right here when you wake. This is our chance to have everything we want," he said and kissed her again. Now that he'd found his way back to her, he'd never let her go.

"We do." She snuggled up to him. In minutes, her breathing evened. Her arm stretched heavy on his belly and she'd twined her legs with his.

He closed his eyes. He had the perfect ending to his day and the best start to the rest of his life. He had the woman of his dreams—his princess.

* * * *

Luke spent the next three months at the castle, getting himself acclimated to the life of a royal. He loved Zara and the time seemed to fly by, but he didn't care. He didn't miss Kenton. Over the first month, he'd retrieved his things, cleaned out the apartment and moved into her suite. Each night he slept beside her and every morning he woke to her in his arms. He'd adjusted to Lysianna well and even managed to score a couple of gallery showings of his work. Zara had her job at the museum and quickly made the collection the best around. Soon, the museum would be open for public tours.

That morning, he woke first and admired her sleeping form. She embodied beauty in slumber. No makeup, her hair in tangles, but she was the prettiest girl. She knew his past and still loved him. He'd bet his parents would've liked her. He wished they could've met her.

"Are you watching me?" She opened her eyes. "I'm a mess."

"You're natural." He kissed her. "I was admiring the view."

"I've got a good view, too." She hugged him. "What's on the agenda for today?"

"I'm planning on spending time in my studio. Ever since Charlie gave me the job of painting Torrance, I haven't been able to accomplish much else. Why? What are you going? Coming to my studio, I hope." He could use mid-afternoon sex. He'd never turn down a chance to be with Zara.

She cuddled up to him. "I will, but I need to do something first." She kissed him, then left the bed.

Luke stretched and rested his hands behind his head. He crossed his ankles. He'd finally come to a good place in his life. He had security, a job creating art and the woman he loved. Next June, he'd marry her. "When is Charlie's official coronation?" he called. "Did they set a date yet?"

"The fifteenth, I believe." She remained in the bathroom. "It won't be Torrance beside him."

"No?" He thought Torrance and Charlie were a good team and had a solid relationship. "They've hit Quitsville already? I thought they were getting serious. What happened?"

"Torrance asked for money and wanted to be declared a duke. He bragged to his friends that he was doing a prince and would end up being the queen. Him, a commoner, would help run the country. I didn't think it was funny, but Charlie hated that he'd been used. Torrance didn't love him and apparently had a boyfriend on the side. Who does that?"

"Your stepmother," Luke said. "I'm sorry to hear about Charlie and Torrance."

"It's for the better. Charlie needs people he can depend on around him." She emerged from the bathroom. "Are you set on marrying in June?"

"I'd marry you today," he said. "The royal protocols declare I can't, but who needs rules?" He rolled onto his side. "Why? Do you want to rush it?"

She crossed the room. "I might." She held something in her hands. "When I left for college, I had a list. I don't remember all the things that were on it. I know one was wanting to be kissed properly."

He curled his fingers behind her head and eased her close. "Like this?" He feathered his mouth over hers until she opened to him, then he sucked on her tongue. She whimpered. When he broke the connection, pink infused her cheeks.

"Like that." She remained close. "I wanted to see a concert, too, but most of all I wanted to have sex with a handsome man and lose my virginity." She traced the seam of his mouth with her finger. "I also wanted to meet the tall, dark and handsome artist downstairs."

"Me?" He feigned shock. "Hello, my name is Luke."

"Zara." She blushed deeper. "I wanted to model for you and be one of those girls in your apartment."

"You're the only one." He smoothed a lock of her hair between his fingers. "What else?"

"I wanted to attend a party—not in the way Corinne threw it, but whatever." She smiled. "Mostly, I wanted to fall in love."

"Have you?" He knew the truth, but adored when she got flustered. "Do you love me?"

"I do, which is why I'm thinking about the wedding. We should move it up." She offered up the item. "We're pregnant."

He stared at her. He'd heard the words and what she said made sense. Pregnant. "Zara?"

"We've been going at it every day and not using protection. It was bound to happen." She crawled onto his lap. "I haven't had my period for the last month and this one is late, too. Is my knight in shining armor having second thoughts?"

He opened and closed his mouth, but no sound came out. He still couldn't wrap his mind around her declaration. Pregnant. She moved the pregnancy test to his hands. He stared at the screen on the stick. A bright pink plus sign. She hadn't been kidding. He met her gaze. "You just took this, didn't you?"

"I did." She folded her hands on his lap. "Are you upset?"

"No." He tugged her down for a kiss. "It's still sinking in, but I'm thrilled. A baby. We're having a baby."

"Our baby." She stretched out on top of him. "You're happy?"

"Very." He held her. "A royal baby." He paused. "Are *you* happy?"

"Yes," she murmured. "Marry me as soon as we can so my life will be perfect and our child will be official."

"It's already official." He stroked her back. "How about we get married tomorrow?" He'd do it now, but he wanted to do this right. They needed some time to get her dress, his tuxedo, flowers, the chapel and the church to officiate. Plus, they'd have to round up Corinne, Elise, Charlie and the king to witness their union.

"It sounds perfect." She tossed the test onto the nightstand. "If I'd known running away would get me the experience I needed to be a better royal and brought me to you, I would've done it earlier. I was bound to move beyond the court. The world had plans for me and I needed to take the chance. If I'd stayed here, I wouldn't have you."

"Things happen when they do for a reason." He brushed her hair from her face. "This is the right time for us."

"Yes, it is." Passion flickered in her eyes. "I love you."

"I love you, too." He kissed the woman he adored. "My runaway royal."

She smiled and rubbed on his growing erection. "I'm all yours."

Now they'd have forever together to grow the love they shared and raise their family. The runaway royal wasn't running any longer—with the love of her life beside her, she'd come home.

Want to see more from this author? Here's a taster for you to enjoy!

Her Man
Wendi Zwaduk

Excerpt

Trouble. That's what most women were — too much trouble! When Logan Malone's last movie had ended, so had his love life. He'd decided women weren't worth the effort — not right now.

Well, no, that wasn't the case — not entirely. Red-hot American blood still charged through his veins and he needed a woman, someone soft in all the right places, tough as nails and unafraid to fight to warm his bed. Why not go for totally impossible?

Logan shifted in his seat. The olive-colored plastic creaked and scratched against the ceramic tile floor. The other three men in the drafty room glared as though he'd ruined their concentration.

"Quiet," the blond man to his right growled.

"Sorry," Logan muttered. He caressed the worn cover of the book jacket as he convinced himself he could play the romantic lead better than the rest of the competition sitting in the drab hallway. Who else could embody the sexy, romantic boy-next-door role better than Romeo Malone, the hunk of the silver screen? He smiled, but quickly lost faith. He faced the biggest roadblock of his career — convincing the directors, producer and author that he was the man for the job. Yeah, another impossible task.

He sighed. Was he the man? Logan took a deep breath to relax before another glance at his competition. Mark Lanigan stood hunched in the corner with his index finger in his ear as he spoke on his cell phone. *Shit.*

Logan flexed his jaw and turned away. His heart dropped to his stomach with a sickening thud. Mark Lanigan wasn't a slouch in the looks department. His baby blues melted even the iciest of hearts with ease. Romance publishers begged for his services as a cover model and Mark had the honor of being selected the 'Sexiest Man of the Decade' according to *Delish* magazine. Last year the man had won an award for his performance of a baseball phenom in love with a farmer's daughter in *Flowers in the Outfield.*

Logan ground his teeth. He should've had that role, but no! He'd spent the two-week casting call screwing around with Katrina Butterfield, romping in the Virgin Islands, answering her darned booty call and living up to his womanizing Romeo image. When he realized he'd forfeited his chance at the part of the year, he'd just about wrung her pretty little neck. He sighed. At least he'd learned from his misstep.

Logan gripped the unforgiving black rubberized armrests. He had to get his career in order. Andrew Speedle exited the conference room through the thick wooden auditorium door. Logan's heart plummeted to the floor. *Great.* More competition he didn't need. Andrew's crooked smile could be both sinister and sweet at the same time. His rumpled, straight-out-of-bed look graced the covers of countless magazines. And he was only twenty-seven! Not only that—he had three supporting roles under his belt, with a lead coming up at the end of the year. Audiences had flocked to see his last film, making it the third highest grossing movie of the year. Andrew could play the sexy hunk-next-door role in his sleep and Logan hated him for it.

Logan pinched the bridge of his nose. Shit. Another part down the drain and he hadn't even tried out yet.

Please let them turn him down. I can do this.

"Malone? Are you giving in already?"

Logan's gaze met Andrew's glare. "They laughed at your sappy credits, didn't they?"

Andrew gave him the finger. "Piss off, Malone. Once she finds out you've screwed the producer and the director, that writer will have your balls in her pocket. Go home and try for a fitting job, something you can handle without dialogue. This ain't the role for you."

Logan's eyes narrowed. "Thanks, asshole."

Andrew sauntered away. Jealousy crashed in Logan's body like a tidal wave. What did that man have that he didn't? He mentally tallied his own assets—broad shoulders, six-pack abs, toned legs and tight buns. Women drooled over his hazel eyes and perfect grin, and he looked hot with any hairstyle. So what was the issue? He was the man for the job without a doubt—case closed.

He sighed. That line of reasoning worked, but Andrew had roles and money, lots of money. A tight ass meant nothing without dollars in the bank.

He thumbed through the book. There were no answers in the battered pages, but simply holding the paperback gave him comfort. He could identify with the hero who wanted true love and honesty with no pretensions. He shook his head. That wasn't possible in Hollywood. Maybe not even in California. Possibly not the world.

Logan flipped to the black and white picture of the author on the inside back cover of the book. Her dowdy professional clothing covered her figure and she smiled sweetly over her shoulder. He'd stared at her so many times and dragged the book around so much over the past three months that the edges of the paper had ruffled. He wondered if she was the actual writer or a model meant to trick the reader. Women that beautiful didn't write romance. Or did they?

Desire curled in his stomach. If she weren't a model, he'd love to tangle his fingers in her dark hair, kiss her lips raw and make her scream with pleasure. Did her skin feel as soft as it looked? Logan guessed it would and she'd do just fine as his arm candy for the premiere. Hell, he'd love to love her for quite a long time.

Love? Too bad it was all a load of crap and nothing more than an act of foreplay involving fictitious emotions. Who actually believed in love? Logan drew a deep breath and let it slide between his lips. He'd never meet a woman who could change his mind and his heart. Women like that didn't exist. Not that lasting relationships mattered much. Paying the bills — that was important. Keeping up the movie star lifestyle had drained his already dwindling bank account. Another flop would mean the end of his career. Career over before the age of thirty-three, hard to envision…but it looked like a very real possibility.

Maybe it was time to go home. No, he'd begged too long and hard to get the chance for the audition. He couldn't back down now. *I will earn this role.*

"Malone?"

Jostled back to reality, Logan looked up. His throat constricted at the sight of another ex. Perfect. "Well, hello, Nikita. It's a pleasure to see you again. Is it my turn, or did you fill the role? I saw Speed walk out earlier."

Nikita Cline pushed her black-rimmed cat's eye glasses back up the bridge of her nose. "It's your turn. We haven't made a decision, yet, but you might do."

Logan felt her heated gaze travel the length of his body. He shivered. He should switch to a different production—one without Nikita. He pasted a wolfish grin on his face and stood to meet her in the doorway. "Well, I'd better dazzle your socks off, then, shouldn't I?"

She grabbed his arm before he entered the room. "You could dazzle other things off instead." Her lips grazed his ear. "I miss you."

Logan shivered again as her perfume wafted to his nose, demanding his undivided attention. He didn't miss the arguments, the accusations, the experimentations she loved so much. She liked to play the field with multiple partners, toys, role-play and whatever she could find for kink. He liked a little kink, but she wasn't his style. "How about I just pass the audition, huh?"

He spotted the women at the table and pasted on his most wicked smile. His voice caught in his throat and a ripple of excitement ran the length of his spine at the sight of his audience. The writer? Was she really there? Or did she moonlight as a screenwriter? Maybe a friend of the producers? *Oh, my, my, my.*

Nikita gestured to the table. "I'd like to introduce the heads of this production. This is Maggie Bowles, our associate producer." She shrugged a shoulder to the woman on the right. "And this is the writer, Cass Jensen."

Logan forced a nod. Maggie had worked on *Break* and co-directed *Maia*, both mega box office hits. She had a reputation for fairness and impartiality with her actors and crew. But the other woman — oh man. He blinked. Cass Jensen penned *Wrong Turn, Slingshot* and toyed with his fantasies from the safety of a black and white photo. Crossbeam Studios had translated three of her earlier novels into box office hits. Now she sat across the room, in living color and completely unaware of his innermost desires.

Had the heat just kicked on? He licked his lips. Something had happened and not just between his legs.

It seemed as if everyone else in the cavernous conference room had evaporated except him and Cass. She wasn't his normal blonde model-type, quite the opposite. She had curves and porcelain skin. Her dark chocolate-colored hair glittered slightly under the harsh glare of the fluorescent lighting, and she brushed the silky strands off her face, revealing her lack of a wedding ring.

Score!

Her mouth curled into a faint smile, accompanying the sparkle in her startling blue-gray eyes. Color rushed into her pale cheeks.

Oh man.

Logan's eyes slipped greedily over her body. Would she flush during sex? The light scent of her perfume muddled his brain. Lilac? Rose? Whatever it was, it was enticing. Logan swallowed hard. Tightness invaded his chest. Such a rapid reaction to a woman knocked him for a complete loop. Cass was the kind of woman who ended up being a cherished lover, not a plaything. He glanced at her once more. His throat went dry. Damn, if she blushed too much longer, he'd be in trouble. If he got time alone with her, he'd be a goner. How would her hands feel gliding along his body? Heaven, probably.

Home of Erotic Romance

Sign up for our newsletter and find out about all our romance book releases, eBook sales and promotions, sneak peeks and FREE romance books!

About the Author

Wendi Zwaduk is a multi-published, award-winning author of more than one-hundred short stories and novels. She's been writing since 2008 and published since 2009. Her stories range from the contemporary and paranormal to BDSM and LGBTQ themes. No matter what the length, her works are always hot, but with a lot of heart. She enjoys giving her characters a second chance at love, no matter what the form. She's been the runner up in the Kink Category at Love Romances Café as well as nominated at the LRC for best contemporary, best ménage and best anthology. Her books have made it to the bestseller lists on Amazon.com and the former AllRomance Ebooks. She also writes under the name of Megan Slayer.

Wendi loves to hear from readers. You can find her contact information, website details and author profile page at https://www.totallybound.com